Dead Man's Trail

Martin Hill Ortiz

Massachusetts
Springfield • Gloucester
©2014

Cover Art by Filip Radulescu
(http://labaiute.deviantart.com/)
Format and Design by D.G. Sutter

ISBN: 978-0-9883146-1-0
Printed in the United States of America
Seven Archons

The desert dogs made a shambles of their meal. A lamb, plump with wool, lay toppled on its back, four hooves saluting the heavens. A wide splash of blood painted its grimy coat; its chewed-up entrails scribbled across the sandy soil. Those guts continued to squirm beneath the Arizona sun, not knowing they were dead. Locked in an eternal stare, the lamb's eyes knew death. Free of gloss, the eyes possessed the brimstone-yellow of a mist-veiled moon. Blowflies hopped around a dribble of its snot.

In his prime, Smith—a fierce border collie— would have never allowed the coyotes near the flock. Now, half-deaf, he had taken up arguing with night owls, a hobby that left him with little sleep and no energy for the day watch. Stiff and oblivious, he stood guard atop a rise that overlooked the flock, awaiting a command from his master.

Asa Powell lined up one of the predators in his rifle's sights, but his horse, Tristan, stammered with his feet. The barrel wandered and the bullet drilled the ground in the middle of the pack, spitting dirt over their paws. The pack swiveled their heads in unison toward the direction of the rifle blast. Then in no apparent hurry they pranced away, abandoning their feast as though killing had been their only goal.

Asa and Tristan headed down to the fallen lamb with Smith taking up the rear. Nearing sixty, working this rough land had kept Asa fit. At the same time, working this miserable land was killing him. He dropped down from his mount, cricked his spine, and tipped back his hat. As he stooped, his legs buckled and gravelly pebbles stabbed his knees. He could use the lamb's carcass to stitch a coat for use as barter at the trading post; its meat would make winter's jerky for the shed. *There've been too many attacks*, he thought, *too much tanning and curing*.

Smith snuffled up and sniffed the bowels. He looked to his master.

Asa unsheathed his skinning knife. Sinking his hand into the belly's gash, he seized hold of one end of the viscera and snipped it clean. He repeated this for the other end, pulling out, piling the intestines in a heap. The guts gave off a sweet, sick smell.

Asa stood, wiped the blood on his chaps, and headed to his saddlebag. He took a shaker out and peppered the entrails with strychnine, then heaved the gutted creature onto Tristan's back.

Three riders appeared atop the ridge. The middle one waved a rifle over his head. "Aces!" he called out.

Tristan shuddered and stamped. Asa gave them a passing glance and returned his concentration to securing the sheep to horseback. "Hey, Tom. I'm hearing ya."

"We're needing a tracker," Sheriff Nickols yelled.

Asa considered turning his back, hopping on top of Tristan and taking off at a quick trot. "Don't suppose you can see I'm busy?"

The three horses with their mounts began

scrambling down the slope. They pulled to a stop near Asa. Thack, Tom, and Nickols posted in three points around him.

"We need you," the sheriff said. "Nobody knows the hills like you." He was as old as Asa, but chubby and bald.

"There could be a pretty coin," Tom added. He had a child's face, its youth accented by his inability to grow a beard. His hat was one size too large and sat squeezed down to his jutting ears. He leaned back in his saddle as though tipping in a chair.

Gummy sheep's blood still clung to Asa's hands. He rubbed in some dirt. "I'm worn down, used up, and don't care."

"It's Coffin Jack," the sheriff said.

That got Asa's attention. "Coffin Jack? You may well say it's a ghost."

"He killed the Barkers," Nickols said. "Butchered them in their home. Thack seen'm."

Thack clutched his breath, the color draining from his ruddy face. "Yeah, I seen 'm. He rode out from the Barkers' place atop a chestnut horse, big and tall. He wore a parson's hat, flat-brimmed and wide, dressed up all in black like a circuit preacher."

"Was he Apache?" Asa asked, for that had been the rumor.

"Never got a look at his face."

"If you saw his face, he'd a seen you," the sheriff said, "and if he'd a seen you, you'd be dead."

While Thack and the sheriff appeared shaken, Tom smacked on his chaw, excited, eager. "We're thinking he dresses like a preacher to get folks' trust, trick them for an invitation into their homes."

Asa reflexively opened and closed his hands, exercising his fingers, tickling a memory. "Or else," he said, "there was this gunslinger in Texas who wore a black preacher's hat, its brim cocked down, his head dipped so nobody could see his face. But all-the-while that devil was watching his rival, feet to holsters. He slowly lifted his hand, as though to tip back his hat, and this got his victim's attention, who was tracking that hand and thinking he was about to meet the devil's eyes. All-the-while he should have been paying proper attention to the other hand, which was doing the shooting."

"Maybe that gunman is Coffin Jack," Nickols said.

"Can't be," Asa replied. "I killed him."

Smith nosed up against his master. Asa sunk a hand down to scratch his scruff. "Nobody's seen Coffin Jack—nobody alive. How can you know it was him?"

"Same as always," the sheriff said. "He killed the family for no good reason. He did his close work with a hatchet. He left an *IOU*."

Asa grunted. *It had to be Jack.*
With resignation he asked, "What did it say?"

"*I, O, U, one hed.*"

"Dan Barker's head was gone!" Tom said, barely containing his excitement. "Neck whacked through at the stump!"

"Aces, why is it no one catches Coffin Jack?" the sheriff asked.
Then, not waiting for an answer, he said "'Cause they ain't seen him 'for a description. By the time they commence hunting, the trail's gone cold. This time we eyeballed him heading east. Only way he could go is to take the gulch...we know where he's headed,

what clothes he's wearing and we seen his horse."

"Chestnut—big and tall," Thack repeated, "with a patch of white on its rump...and a saddle blanket, no saddle."

Nickols nodded. "If he makes it to the hills, we'll need you to flush him out, and if we cross paths with a party of natives, we need you to speak their tongue."

"We got hand irons to secure him for jail," Thack said. Left unspoken was the account of how Coffin Jack had worked himself free of his ropes and slaughtered the last lawman unlucky enough to catch him.

"Or else we'll string him up right where we find him," Tom said. The long golden coils of a virgin lariat were hitched to his saddle. "The bounty is all the same, dead or alive."

All were quiet now, looking to Asa, waiting on his answer. His pulse no longer felt his own, now beating with a communal vengeance. "I'll need to pen my flock," he said at last. "I'll set them straw and water for a couple of days, but that's the most I can promise."

"Sure thing, Aces." The sheriff broke into a smile. "With you as our tracker, Jack ain't got a chance. You're half Injun."

Asa cocked a scornful eye at Nickols.
"Now, I'm just saying you got Injun sense."

Asa grinned, surprised that his friend flustered so easily. "You offended me because you think I'm only half."

The sheriff laughed. "All-righty. Two days you'll give us. Two days is aplenty."

Thack nodded along with the sheriff, saying, "That's all I'm in for. I'm stopping by my place to collect my Henry Repeater and pass word to Sharon, so she don't go launching a second posse to hunt me down. We're joining up next to the spring at the mouth of Liar's Gulch in a couple of hours."

"If Jack makes it into the hills, we got a demanding task ahead," the sheriff said. "We got to nab him afore then, quick."

"But don't tell no one," Thack said. "If'n they hear Coffin Jack's out there, we'll have packs of bounty grubbers in the crossfire, all itching for the reward. On top of that...a squad of soldiers will swarm down from Fort Henry, shoving us aside and making a ruckus. They'll spook Jack so that he'll never get found."

"Two days," Asa repeated.

Asa hoped that with Smith penned up with the sheep, the dog would concentrate on his duties and not spend the better share of his day lost to shut-eye. He knew the owls would keep Smith vigilant at night. He had no time to skin or cure the fallen lamb. Since he could hardly leave the temptation of rotting meat close by his pen, he packed the carcass to take with him, until he could drop it somewhere distant.

His best firearm was a Winchester carbine, a short-barreled rifle good for close fights and medium range sniping. It took the same bullets as the handgun he packed. He grabbed a pair of army canteens and strung a set of hollow gourds across his horse's backside. If Asa wasn't careful, the full bore of the sun's heat kicking off the lava rock would fry his brain surely as lazing his head on a breakfast skillet. In the wrong places there was no shade for miles and no water for a day.

He didn't pack food. He could live for two days without sustenance. If he was to get caught up in the chase, his hunger would kick him as a reminder to head home. *I should have said no*, he thought. *The blood-fury, this hunting humans, is for the young.*

Even those creatures that thrive on scorched land hated days like these. The sun grew fiercer as it tilted to the west, so that by three o'clock the desert rat preferred to plunge the depths of a snake hole, over baking in the miserly shade of a creosote. By the time it turned four, Tristan and Asa were perched on a bluff overlooking Nix's Hollow. Down below—amid a stretch of barren red clay—Liar's Gulch bloomed with a burst of green, a copse of spiky trees and cottonwoods. Beyond that was a puzzle of sharply cut sandstone hills, dappled with flows of black lava rock and sprinkled with volcanic ash. Farther so were the desolate Gila Mountains.

Four hours of daylight remained; the night would be moonless. Coffin Jack preferred attacking on the days of new moons, then hurrying off to blend in with the nightfall. A distant storm cloud crawled in front of the sun, dragging with it a shadow as large as the valley below. Asa took a swig from his canteen, swishing water over the dust in his mouth, washing up a viscous sludge and swallowing hard.

He shucked the lamb's carcass from the back of his horse. Maybe he could retrieve it on his way back (if he returned before the bird and insect scavengers took occasion to feast). Tristan and Asa ambled down the slope.

After a funeral in Tucson, the townsfolk began asking what had become of the local coffin-maker—a friend of the deceased and someone who surely would have attended the service. The first indication that something horrid had occurred came when the body of the man who was supposed to have been buried was found on the outskirts of town, propped against a tree stub with a note pinned to his chest:

I,O,U, one ded boddy.

A group of anxious citizens dug up the recently interred pine box. There they found the coffin-maker, bound and gagged, suffocated after being buried alive. Arguments ensued over who could have done such a thing. The Apaches were suspected (regularly blamed for every calamity from cattle raids to drought); others declared the crime was nothing like those of the Indians. The Apaches would never taunt by writing an *IOU*. They sometimes mocked the living, but always respected the dead.

Over the following months, five more killings took place, including one among the Chiricahua tribe. Some settlers disputed that incident by claiming the Indians were misdirecting the white folk, trying to garner sympathy and dodge blame for their own foul deeds. Over the course of his killings, Jack had outmaneuvered all of his pursuers: posses, cavalry, and Apache. The demand for his capture became the one uniting force among the local warring factions.

———————————

During much of the year, the spring at Liar's Gulch gurgled with health. It leaked out from a horizontal crack in the cliff's side and dribbled down to form a mushy tract of sand and a small pond in which cattails sprouted. In this season of thirst, all that remained was a moist slick of rock, the water collecting in a mucky puddle. Throughout the year, a grove drank from its deeper wells; along with a pair of tall cottonwoods grew smaller chinaberries, sycamores, and ashes.

A slender trail cut through the juniper scrub, leading to the amphitheater of trees. Along that path, Tom's horse trotted up to block Tristan and Asa's progress. Its saddle sat lopsided, its saddle buckle cut. Tristan nosed up to the horse, backing the creature away until it stood in a clearing.

In a patch of shade, three bodies hung from the branch of a skeletal sycamore. Sheriff Nickols dangled neck-in-noose, the rope looped over the branch and tied to a buckle in the tree's root, his arms drooping loosely at his sides. Tom's hands were tied behind his back—his boyish face a plump and ghastly purple. In between the two other victims, Thack was strung up by his wrists, the chain of his manacles looped over the branch. His lips had been sewn shut and a torn strip of cloth was pinned to his chest with his deputy's badge:

I,O,U...

Asa moved in closer.

I,O,U, 2 Is.

Thack's body heaved with a sudden convulsion, his chest bucking, his lips ripping at their stitches, gasping for air. His eyelids sprung open, revealing empty sockets.

"Thack, it's me, Aces," the tracker said.

Thack choked on the pink foam that sputtered between his sutured lips, his words furious and hoarse. "Tell Sharon. Tell Sharon, I'm sorry. I'm sorry, I broke my promise."

A fountain of bloody tears flooded and spilled from the hollows of his eyes.

Asa considered how to cut the man down. Since it would take forever to saw through the hand irons, this left the option of either hacking the thick tree limb or cutting Nickols down to drag Thack to the end of the branch. Then, with a deeper horror, Asa asked himself, "How did they get there? How could Jack string up all three?"

Thack had ridden to his home, meaning Nickols and Tom arrived first. Coffin Jack would have seen the two and recognized the need to take out Nickols before the kid. Tom's saddle belt was severed. Jack must have figured the kid would panic and ride off. A surprise attack took place after the two had dismounted.

Asa tugged on Nickols's boot, swiveling his body. The back of his head showed the deep cleft of a hatchet wound. The sheriff was attacked from behind, killed before he was hung. Then, Jack got a bead on Tom—tying the boy's hands at gunpoint—and finished by stringing him up.

The rope leading to the sheriff's body was frayed near its base, the bands of twine halfway split. When Thack arrived, he tried to cut the sheriff down. That left Thack vulnerable. Yet, why was Thack dying? Asa looked at Thack's belly, his shirt tugged up with the agony of his distended arms. Peeking out from between the stretch of his buttons was a wide swath of gauze. Through the gauze, through the shirt was a bloom of red, and on the ground by the rope's anchor, a splotch of blood.

Coffin Jack shot Thack when he tried to cut down

the sheriff, then dressed his wound, replaced his shirt, manacled him, gouged his eyes, and sewed his lips shut before stringing him up. Thack was left alive to lure Asa in, his eyes gone and lips sealed so that he couldn't see Asa approaching, and thus shout a warning. Thack was a worm dangling on a hook. Thack was bait. Asa would be attacked when he tried to take Thack down from the tree. He was being watched.

He didn't move, his eyes scanning for sniper's nests or a flash of a man in black. Thack had taken a bullet front side. A low angle meant the oak brush, a high angle, the brink of the cliff. For the latter, it would have taken too long for Jack to scramble down. Thack, only wounded, would have left a trail of blood crawling to a safer spot.

The brush oak stretched out to a crop of boulders. The rocks were thick with shadows, but empty of visible targets. From his current position, Asa would probably get one shot free before being picked off in the open. He needed to retreat. He drew a mental path back to Tristan, one that would be out of the line of fire, and casually followed.

After tying Tristan to some scrub stalks, he retrieved a buck-knife from its saddle-scabbard and collected some extra ammo from his leather pack. He also took a canteen. With a quick pivot he shot Thack in the chest—ending his friend's misery—and scurried to the cliffside wall, where he crouched behind a boulder near the spring.

There he waited, and could wait for days. He had all of the water necessary to survive. If Jack came out to attack, he would be exposed in the open. Jack might wait until night to try an ambush, but absolute darkness made for a difficult approach and, to draw near, Jack would first need to scratch his way through the oaks, wherein Asa would hear him coming.

Asa laid out the extra bullets, each spaced a finger's-width for quick retrieval. He took long, luxurious gulps from his canteen, gargling loudly, letting his foe know how thoroughly his thirst had been sated. The skim of water from the spring did not allow for an easy refill. Asa sopped a rag in the seepage and wrung it into the mouth of his canteen, repeating this again and again—filthy tears slowly replacing what he'd drank.

Two hours passed.

A distant, lone coyote whimpered. In Asa's imagination it was the cry of an infant. He invoked the name of his son.

The steep walls of the gulch presented Coffin Jack with two choices: he could retreat up into the ravine and on the sandstone hills or he could come out to play. If he was to choose the ravine, he'd need to cross a short clearing through which Asa would have a clean shot. Any escape attempt would need to start before night fell. In darkness the labyrinthine paths, chancy footholds, and deep crevices of the sandstone hills made for a lethal passage.

Not being tied down, the horses of Nickols, Tom, and Thack were able to dawdle about nosing the ground, hunting down and gobbling up clumps of grass. Tristan—tied up, hungry, and far from the food—grew impatient.

Asa steadied his emotions, fighting back a blood-rage, trying to direct his mind elsewhere, away from the ghastly images of his friends' corpses. He exorcised the face of Thack's wife from his thoughts, returning the full bore of his concentration to the boulders beside the scrub-oak.

Coffin Jack is not a fighter. He killed the weak and waylaid the rest. He must have tied his horse off somewhere up the ravine. That's where he would head—and soon, before the light faded.

From the shadows came a peeping whistle. Thack's horse took note, shuffling closer to the sound's source, disappearing from Asa's view. Asa wriggled his back against the cliff wall, working up to peek over the boulder, laying his rifle barrel across its top, steadying it, taking aim at the clearing. Thack's horse loped back into sight. It took Asa a moment to notice the two extra legs.

Asa fired to frighten the horse and free up an unobstructed shot. From both the rifle's blast and a bullet whizzing past its ear, Thack's horse reared and bounded into a frenzied gallop. Behind the horse, Jack's grips held tight to the saddle horn and beneath its belt. At first the killer pedaled with his feet, and was then dragged into the mouth and down the gullet of the ravine. Asa rushed into the clearing, firing again, wasting a bullet.

He hurried up to the first bend, hugging the wall and peeking around the corner. Thack's horse lay in the sand, its neck jerking and blood gushing from its slit throat. Asa trotted to the next turn. Ahead was an empty tract between fifty yards of high walls. Hoof prints in the sand said that Jack had met his horse and took off fast.

Asa ran back, leapt atop Tristan, whipped the loop off his hitch, and launched into the shadows of the narrow ravine. He charged full speed through a dozen twists, one arm extended and his six-shooter ready to blaze, desperate to catch Jack before he climbed into the hills.

Up ahead the canyon split in two. Asa pulled to a halt. He knew this area. The hoof prints of Jack's horse led to the right, where the gulch soon narrowed into a dead end surrounded by steep fifteen foot walls. By taking that direction, Jack had become cornered in a place without recess or rock for shield. Unless...Coffin Jack also knew this place. The hoof prints in the sand entering this dead end route appeared tightly spaced, as though the horse had begun a casual walk. If Jack had abandoned his horse and sent it off, down the cul-de-sac, then he was inviting Asa to enter. When Asa took the bait, Jack would come up behind him. Asa would be easy pickings.

No tracks headed up the other branch. Still, Asa was certain Jack had gone that way on foot, scrabbling from rock to rock to leave no trace. Asa rode up the left-hand branch at a cautious pace, eyeing each corner for a sniper's nest. Twilight reigned. Shadows spilled out from behind the rocks—swallowing the canyon, obscuring the path ahead. Above, along the rim, the gathering gloom of night transformed the silhouettes of tall boulders into the idols of discarded gods. Asa imagined any of those boulders could come alive. Any of them could be Jack.

This fork of the ravine ended in a bowl-like depression, its slopes soft and sandy. Trying to lead Tristan through the dusk on up this crumbly incline would risk his horse's life and slow Asa down, so he dismounted. He scrambled up the side, hands and feet clawing at the red clay, surveying the way forward with his hands. Once atop the edge he could see to the distant horizon, where a yellow blazing splinter marked the farewell of the sun. The miserly sum of light cast by the slurry of stars offered nothing to illuminate the way ahead.

A hundred yards to the east, Asa made out the

figure of a man dressed in black—Coffin Jack, his figure squeezed and distorted by the darkness, a broomstick scarecrow, his arms unnaturally long, his back crossed by a holstered rifle. Jack's arms rose, seemingly in surrender, then he dropped out of view, down a crevice. Asa ran up to its edge. Below him was the cul-de-sac, the other branch of the ravine. From out of that emptiness, a horse nickered. A matchstick bloomed as Jack lit a slender cigarette. In the spotlight of the match, Asa saw Jack's other hand, the one raising a gun. Asa dropped against the canyon's lip as the gun blasted.

Asa scrambled to his feet. Backtracking, he skidded down the sandy slope to where he came upon a nervous Tristan. He led his horse by hand through the cavernous world of the pitch-black canyon, the grit of the dry river sand under his boots his only guide. The darkness had become so complete that Asa couldn't know whether or not Jack was an arm's length away. Asa stopped to listen for footsteps or a tumbling stone. He heard a steady chirr of beetles and the sinuous sound of bottle flies diving and rising about Tristan in a spastic orbit. Tristan's heavy breath percolated through his bit. A howl from a coyote sounded close enough that Asa imagined it ready to leap down upon him.

He felt about for a scrub pine to hitch Tristan, encountering one that sprouted from the crumble of the canyon wall.

Asa skimmed his fingers along the side of the canyon, making a turn at the fork in the ravine, leading to the dead end.

Somewhere up ahead, hooves scuffed against

sand. Asa crept forward, keeping to the canyon wall. As he neared the dead end, he saw the dancing glow of campfire painting the sandstone wall in orange, stretching the shadow of Jack's mount into a form as tall as the horse of Troy. Asa raised his six-shooter and steadied himself against the wall, finger on the trigger, thumb crushing the hammer, awaiting a target. He kept his fingers motionless, even the click of cocking might give away his approach.

In one corner, a stinger of light speared the darkness—the tip of a cigarette. Its glimmer did not illuminate a face or hand. Asa studied the ember carefully, looking for an up and down twitch of lips or the flare that comes with a drag. The cigarette never wavered or flickered, its fiery ash slowly lengthening. It was another trap. A cigarette could sit anywhere. If Asa was to fire, the flash of his gun would announce exactly where he stood.

Asa retreated, moving slower than the shallow breath that leaked between his rounded lips; his muscles were so tense they felt ready to tear free of the bone.

He exited the dead end, backed into a tight nook in the gulch, and crouched to sit. In the great empty darkness, he concentrated on whether or not his eyes were open.

On a moonless night like this when Asa was five, and Western Missouri was a borderland of lawless and drunken towns, a crowd of torch-bearers visited his parents' home. Painted as Indians, the mob called on Asa's father, demanding that he'd return the river.

With the high-water floods that spring, the town's stream redrew its course. Where it once fed the ditches of many a farm it now wove only through the Powell's homestead. Even with a musket barrel planted under his chin, Asa's father refused to let his neighbors dam and re-route the creek, instead insisting they pay for their water at a usurious price.

The villagers expected no for his answer. They killed Asa's father and mother, later telling the other townsfolk it was an Indian raid. At an inquest Asa testified they were not Indians, that he knew the difference between painted white folk and natives. He pointed to grand jury members who were there that night, but he was a child of five and persuaded no one.

Asa's six-month-old brother was adopted by the family of one of the killers. They sent Asa to a St. Louis orphanage where he stayed until he turned twelve, at which time he stowed away on a wagon train to Texas.

...the slender light of pre-dawn caught Asa by surprise. He had been sleeping. The dark and his dreams had fused, but for how many hours, he didn't know. The once black sky was now a sooty gray, daubed free of stars by daybreak.

Asa could again see his hands and feet. He loped over to the junction and studied the tracks in the sand. Foot and hoof prints led away from the cul-de-sac, back down to the entry of Liar's Gulch. Jack had reversed directions, returning to the spring.

Asa checked the dead end where Jack had stayed the night, looking for pieces of the story. He studied Jack's boot prints in the sand. Sharp-toed, one boot had a pocket where the leather had worn through at the forefoot. The tip of the boot dug into the sand, its end seeming to bend as though he wore boots several sizes too large. The horse's hoof prints showed seven nails—unusual. Asa could use that to pick out his trail. There were no signs indicating that Jack crouched or slept. The cigarette stub was tobacco wrapped in an oak leaf, Apache-style.

By the time Asa and Tristan arrived at the mouth of the gulch, Jack had come and gone, cutting the throats of the other two horses. The branch holding the three posse members had been hacked through and they lay toppled on the ground. Thack's head was missing.

Coffin Jack had chopped the bodies down to make sure Asa would lag behind, spending his time burying the dead. Asa knew he had no other choice. He could not leave their bodies to the coyotes and buzzards. Jack's ploy gained him the advantage of time and distance, but by taking Thack's head as a prize, Asa had figured out the killer's next destination.

While riding up out of Nix's Hollow, Asa became aware of a shadow spiriting between the tall rocks— a Chiricahuan. Since their forced resettlement, their tribe had been engaged in an on-and-off war against the U.S. and Mexican cavalries, with homesteaders and everyone else in the crossfire. In recent months an uneasy peace prevailed.

This lone scout had traveled far from the reservation. It could be an outlaw or else the lookout for a traveling party. It could mean a friendly chat or an arrow. As she dashed between hiding places, Asa recognized his stalker as Lozen, sister of Chief Victorio. She was a prophet and warrior, often traveling in advance of Geronimo. She and Asa knew each other well. She would not attack, but her extended pursuit seemed curious.

Asa divided people into three groups: Europeans, Indians, and himself. The Europeans called themselves Americans, or Mexicans, or else kept the names of their faraway tribes such as the English or Chinese. They had a long history of war, tribe-fighting-tribe or direction-fighting-direction, North against South.

The realms of the Indians also took on broad titles such as Comanche and Apache and were then further divided into tribes including the Chiricahua, the Mescalero, and Yavapai. They, too, had a long history of war.

Asa was neither of these. Once upon a long time back he had searched these hills for gold and, with that pursuit, a chunk of his life was forever stolen by a fevered dream, lost hunting for a colored rock that was worshiped by those who idolized coins. Asa now saw these as slugs of metal, worthless except in the delusions of their believers. Twenty years of fruitless prospecting in these barren mountains purged the European from his soul. His heart had joined with the earth, the harsh soil where he scrabbled and scratched out his existence. In that sense he'd become Indian—a person connected to this rugged, bitter land.

Yet, he wasn't Indian. He felt no kinship with their battles, forever fighting impossible odds. Years back, when he reached out to them, they let him know he was a stranger.

"Lozen!" he called.

No answer.

"Lozen!" He felt a pang of desperation to talk to her; he hadn't spoken with her tribe for years. The only answer to his call was the rush of wind on stone.

By the time Asa had reached the brink of the hollow, all signs of Lozen had vanished. Perhaps she was still there and better hidden, having successfully blended in with the rocks and shadows, or maybe she journeyed on.

I, O, U, one hed.

Jack had chopped Thack's head off to bring it to the Barkers' ranch and make good on his promissory note. As he approached the Barkers' homestead, Asa saw the effects of the abrupt end of their lives. Cattle were scattered far and near. A bull stood on their porch along with a heavy pile of manure. A goat munched on clothes it had yanked free from the line.

There were no signs that anyone had come here since the murders. Thack insisted they keep quiet, claiming they needed to prevent bounty hunters and the army from joining in the search and spooking Jack. Asa suspected it was just to avoid splitting the reward.

Just before the cave-in, prospectors are always sure they're about to have a lucky strike.

Death by easy money.

Asa paused at the approximate place where Thack would have spotted Jack riding away from the home, fresh from murder. Asa shut his eyes to visualize—a man in a preacher's hat and black coat atop a tall horse. Asa's eyes opened, his face stretched with sudden realization. One thing that Thack hadn't mentioned in his description of Jack: blood. His cleric's frock was used as a cover he could quickly toss over the clothes he used during the slaughter.

Asa rode into the corral where Tristan could have water and hay, and a moment's peace. Jack had proved fond of slashing the throats of horses and by penning him up, Asa would keep his friend far from the bloodshed. Tristan's ribs beat with furious breaths. His eyes spoke of pain and betrayal: pain from the hard ride, betrayal because he was being abandoned before the fight.

Asa strode toward the Barkers' house. The butt of his Winchester carbine was tucked in the crook of his arm, its barrel swaying like a pendulum, its nose grazing the crowns of the desert shrubs. His hand fixed over the trigger guard. He kept his grip tight, ready at a moment's notice to raise the barrel and blast whatever appeared in the windows.

He kicked the door open, scooted back beside the jamb, and waited for a response. After counting to ten he stooped low and ducked in, taking cover behind a wood stove. Once more he counted the silence, measured against the thump of his pulse. He peeked over the wide griddle of the stove lid.

The house consisted of one large room, two cots near the stove, a pair of ladder-back chairs, and a stretched-hide sofa at the distant end. To his side stood a mannequin draped with a swatch of muslin, and stuck full of pins. A tall desk that grew up into a bookcase stood farther on. In a corner beyond that was a dining table set for a meal.

Beautiful in life, horrid in death, the naked corpse of Althea Barker sat propped up, posed, her elbows on the tabletop and fingers bent to grip a fork and knife. Her neck displayed a purple smile; she had been garroted. Maggots dropped from her throat and lips. Set in front of her, Thack's head rested squarely on a plate.

Asa thought the gruesomeness, itself, might be a trap to make him lower his guard for a moment. This house possessed no recesses in which to hide, so he became concerned about someone firing in from outside. His eyes flitted between the windows. While doing this, Asa realized he'd overlooked an elongated lump beneath the blanket that covered one of the cots. Dan Barker's body was missing, but this bundle was hardly large enough to be a child.

He approached it slowly, rifle barrel steady. Ripping back the blanket revealed a split side of beef, fresh from the smokehouse. Pinned to the meat between its ribs was a strip of cloth with scrawled letters:

I, O, U—U.

It was an invitation.

The Barkers' smokehouse was a square stone chimney, ten feet tall and wide, built atop a short rise, a prominence that overlooked the sprawling desert. It had no windows. Its door was propped open by a thick chock of wood. The preacher's hat hung on a peg beside the entrance. Even from a distance, Asa could see inside. A wedge of light revealed smoked slabs of beef hanging from hooks along a metal bar. A rifle barrel peeked out of a crevice between the dangling shanks of meat.

Asa stole up to the side of the smokehouse and crept along the wall. He set aside his carbine and drew his six-shooter, more flexible for close encounters. After coming up to the door, he inspected the preacher's hat—well-worn, its felt balding in patches. The headband was still damp with sweat.

So be it. He would go inside and end this now, face to face. As to who would die, he divided that out into thirds: Coffin Jack, or else Asa, or else both. In two out of three outcomes, Asa was dead. He figured his chances were better here than on the trail, where an ambush or sniper's shot could bring him down.

Asa burst through the door and rolled along the hard dirt floor. He came to a stop and unloaded three shots at the figure behind the slabs of meat. The bullets hit their mark, the man in the shadows shuddering with each strike. Asa paused. The figure pivoted, the toes of its boots skimming the smokehouse floor. Dan Barker's headless corpse hung on the meat rack, a rifle tucked under its arm.

The daylight flamed out as the door slammed shut. Outside, a thud resounded from a heavy wooden crossbar falling in place. Asa rammed his shoulder against the door, which responded with a barely a quiver. The smokehouse was chimney *and* vault, solidly built to turn away both animal and human thieves.

He stepped back, widening his eyes and allowing his pupils to dilate. A square of meshwork in the ceiling vent dropped a tight checkerboard of light, illuminating Dan and a side of beef.

The walls were stone, the floor earthen and hard-packed. A slender hole was carved in one corner of the dirt and covered with a round metal grid. Up through this duct came a roiling stream of smoke, the harsh tang of mesquite. Asa backed away, waving off the fumes. Not long after, the entire chamber was fogged over. His eyes watered, his throat dried. His ribs heaved with each inhalation. He fought against blind panic. With forced calmness, he holstered his gun and took out a cigarillo. Once lit, he drew in a few unhurried drags, blowing smoke into the smoke. He reasoned he had one chance. He flicked his flaming cigarillo to the floor, then grabbed the bar of the meat rack and hoisted himself up.

If this place had any soft spots, it would be the ceiling—a patchwork of rough-hewn timber. He struggled to maintain his balance atop the rack while beating a fist against the ceiling. It rattled, but refused to yield.

Asa repositioned, kicked high, striking the metal grille of the ceiling vent. It popped up and out. Then, with his body at an angle—his perch tenuous and off-balanced, boots skidding against the bar of the meat rack—he managed to fix his shoulder against the wall and squeeze his head through the upper vent. It was too small to allow his shoulders passage, but in this contortion he could breathe and filled his lungs with long, hungry gasps. His soles slipped, but he regained his footing in time.

After a few moments, his head cleared and his eyes stopped streaming. He saw a man in the far distance wearing the clothes of a circuit preacher, speaking to Sharon, Thack's wife. Asa wanted to shout out a warning, but the meat rack collapsed and he plunged to the smokehouse floor. The fumes choked him, surely as hands around his neck. His world turned gray and then black.

-VII-

Asa awoke to find a weed being stuffed in his mouth.

"Chew," Lozen said in Apache. She hovered over him, her mesmeric face etched with a frown, her eyes as sharp and piercing as pins.

The herb felt like ants stinging his tongue. He slapped a numb hand against his cheek, streaking his fingers through a coat of sweat and soot. Asa lay on his back, muscles tingling, his ribcage bucking. He peered through burning eyes, through puddles of tears. Viewing her hazy image, Asa longed to bend up and kiss her—no, not her, a different memory.

"The People got word of these recent killings," Lozen said. "They sent me to follow Coffin Jack, to learn more about the white-eyed demon."

The Apache referred to themselves as N'de, *The People.* They called the intruding settlers and cavalry *white eyes.*

"He's a white eye?"

"The People don't use death boxes and would never name a man "Coffin." He wears the holy clothes of the white eyes' priests."

"He's not a holy man," Asa said. "His clothes are a lie."

"And who among you is not a liar and thief?" she said. "You invaded our lands and your priests declared your God as the mightiest. You shoved us under the river to make our spirits clean. We are not unclean."

Years back, when Asa first met Lozen, she had this same spitting anger. She tolerated him because he had taken a cousin of hers as a bride, Spring Blossom. Then, when the tribe was forced to relocate, the army rejected Asa's plea to let him journey with them. In turn, Spring Blossom refused to abandon her people and stay behind with him. As though Asa's separation from his wife represented some sort of personal triumph, Lozen scolded him, saying, "Your game has ended. Stop playing Indian."

Asa tried to explain he was an Indian, his soul had become one with this land.

"You will not be part of the land until your blood has joined it. The red clay of these mountains holds the blood of generations of The People."

Spring Blossom died one year later when her camp was stricken by cholera. The news launched Asa into a yearlong drinking binge.

———————————

"How is Clement?" Asa asked.

"Sturdy and fearless. We call him Fierce Eye. He lost sight on his right side while fighting with rocks."

"Does he ask about me?"

"He has many fathers."

"Tell him one of his fathers thinks of him."

Tristan snorted and stamped, hocking up a lizard

that he'd swallowed with a clump of grass. The noise roused Asa, who bolted to a sitting position. He spat out the grit that remained from the medicine weed. "Sharon Cade," he said. "Thack's wife."

"Is that the woman who spoke with Coffin Jack?"

"She's in danger. I have to help her." He struggled to his feet.

"She has seen the face of the demon. It will not permit her to live."

"I have to..."

"Go to her," Lozen said, "but don't concern yourself with pursuing Coffin Jack. I am returning to The People to inform them of all that I've witnessed. This demon has also visited death upon us. We will hold counsel to determine The People's course of action, and when we choose revenge, none can spare him."

With a muscular leap, she was astride the back of her horse.

"Lozen!" Asa called as she started to trot away. She pulled her horse to a halt and cocked her ear to the side. "I'm going after Jack," Asa shouted. "If I don't come home, The People can have my sheep."

Her horse's hooves beat a trail of dust as she rode beyond view.

Asa returned to the smokehouse to gather his carbine. It was gone. The damned thing cost more than the shack in which he lived.

The Cade Ranch spread from the bank of the Gila on up through a few well-watered fields, until its fringe became lost in the desert. The broad canopy of an elm shaded its farmhouse. In their reprieve from the sun, chickens pecked at dried cobs long-since stripped of their meaty kernels. A belligerent rooster strutted, tail-feathers held high.

Asa dismounted at a distance, tethered Tristan, and then gave his friend a parting pat on the rump. He split open his six-gun, chucked the empty shells and refilled the chambers. He gave its cylinder a whirl to make sure grit hadn't jammed its spin.

As he strode toward their place, he studied the layout for lines of fire and rifle nests—the tree, the lean-to chicken coop, the farmhouse's windows and its roof. The front door of the farmhouse had a slide panel to greet strangers and a loophole to hold a rifle.

That door was ajar and quivered lightly in the breeze.

Asa plastered himself against a side wall and inched to the porch. He ducked to trot beneath a window, continuing on to the door, where he stooped and listened. A pendulum clock ticked. Some clunking came from a back room. He entered the living room, bent low, then dropped to one knee and swept his six-gun corner to corner.

The living room was as broad as the house. Its back branched off to become a dining room, and down a hall, a kitchen. Two doors led to separate bedrooms, one having been fashioned as a nursery in the days before Sharon lost her child.

The sounds continued—metal spanking metal. Asa slipped into the dining room. The ghastly image of Althea's corpse flooded his memory. A pair of half-emptied cups of coffee rested on the table near a porcelain cream pot. Two flies rehearsed a minuet atop a plate of sugar cubes. On a saucer sat the crushed stub of an oak-leaf cigarette. A pyramid of corn fritters rose above the rim of a serving basket. Asa touched the side of a coffee cup, tepid.

"Aces!" Sharon said, emerging from the kitchen, startling him. She wore a diamond-patterned calico dress. Her hands were coated with flour. She was twenty, beautiful, so tall that it intimidated many a man. She was also flirtatious, pointing her shoulder his way, turning her head to present a playful annoyance. "Don't you know how to knock?"

She seemed more concerned by his lack of manners than by his drawn pistol. She patted her ghostly hands on her apron.

Asa's head sagged low, his lips pursed. He studied

her, trying to decipher the moment. *Why is she alive?*

"You alone?" he asked.

"For a spell now."

"The door was hanging open. I came in." He lowered his gun and set it on the table.

"You got to slam it just so, or it don't stay slammed."

Her eyes appeared innocent of pain and concern. Thack must have told her nothing before he left, naught about the Barkers or the hunt for Coffin Jack. The grim tale of the past two days was an avalanche ready to crash down on her, and Asa was about to start that rockslide.

"Water?" she said. "I got some fresh from the well, so cool it will sweat your glass."

Asa felt as though there was a stone in his throat. He gave a stiff nod.

Sharon tossed a parting smile his way as she headed back into the kitchen.

Asa grabbed a corn fritter, bit into it, gulping down its gritty crumbs. In doing this, he acknowledged the hunger gnawing at his belly. Beneath the hunger lurked a fiercer sensation, one that made him feel empty, as though his bones had been carved hollow and made into whistles. From the void of where his marrow had once been, arose a sharp sting of fury, the birth of an obsession. Whatever it took, he would kill Coffin Jack.

His pulse thumped in his head. From the kitchen came a clatter of pans. Further off, chimes tinkled on the porch, kicked by a breeze. Chickens clucked. A gust of wind ruffled the elm. Nearer by, a clay pot clinked against glass, followed by the gurgle of pouring water.

Sharon returned with two glasses full raised, high enough for toasting. "Thack's been out for a day rounding up some of the Barkers' strays. Grab a seat."

Asa placed his glass on the table and dropped his arms to his side.

"You look spooked," Sharon said. "Did something happen?" Then, "Is it *Thack?*"

"You met a preacher?"

"Yes, I did. I was heading to the Barkers' when I ran into him. He told me they were out. How is Thack?"

"What did he look like?"

"The preacher? Ordinary," she said, "What are you not telling me?"

"Old? Young?"

"Not really. Aces, what happened?"

"Which direction did he head?"

The pace of her speech quickened. "He asked about a saddler; I told him about the Wynne's boy. *Aces?*"

His hand trembled. He raised the water to his lips, taking in just enough to moisten his parched mouth.

He said, "I've got to get you someplace safe. I'll shepherd you up to Solomonville. You'll need to oblige the sheriff there by telling him all you can about the preacher."

"Why not just talk to Nickols?"

Even with the cool water, Asa's throat felt deadly dry. He opened his mouth to speak. No words came. Sharon's eyes spilled over with tears.

At last he said, "Thack...Nickols...Tom

Jenkins...the Barkers...."

Sharon's face drained as he proceeded step-by-step through his funeral march of names. She anticipated the final entry before he spoke it.

"Coffin Jack."

Why was she allowed to live? All others who had seen Jack's face paid with their lives.

Perhaps the reason was to slow Asa down. It worked. At first Sharon screamed, clawed at him, cursing his name, blaming him for failing to protect her husband. Asa tried to restrain her and when that didn't work, tried dodging her wildly swinging fists. When she still refused to abandon her assault, he grabbed her again, this time seizing her wrists and squeezing for so long and so tightly that she wore bruises for bracelets.

Sharon lapsed into silence, dipping her head in defeat. When Asa finally let go, she let fly a single slap, then stormed into the living room. With a chilly calm she began packing a hefty Gladstone bag, cramming some items in, hurling others aside. Asa took the plate of corn fritters, settled on the sofa, and sated his hunger. He listened to her frenzy of stuffing and flinging with closed lids.

When she came upon her vanity table, she used her forearm to sweep all of its clamshells and stoppered bottles into the case. She cracked photos out of their frames and tossed them on top of her already brimming-over suitcase. Sharon gave the contents one final crush, then snapped the case shut.

"I've got a sister in Maley," she said.

Asa knew this was a lie. All of her family lived east of the Mississippi. Maley had a Southern Pacific line, an avenue of flight. She cared nothing about helping to catch Coffin Jack, only to abandon this violent land forever.

"I'll take you there," Asa said—another lie. Each tick of the clock aided Jack's getaway. Asa was determined to haul Sharon along with him in his pursuit. He told himself that he could both track down Jack and protect Sharon. Wynne's Saddlery sat on the edge of Safford. She'd be safe in town.

———————————

Passage was slow. Asa had looped their two mounts together, worried she was so distracted that she might drift away. Or maybe she'd recognize his plan and bolt off. The sun was crazy-hot. Rattlers refused to peek out of their holes. A vulture hid, tucked in the shadow of a saguaro. Asa peppered her with more questions about the preacher, but she said nothing.

"I lost my wife, you know," Asa said.

"So Thack told me. But she was just an Indian."

Asa pretended to have never heard her remark; she was in pain. He calmly recounted the tale of the past day: how their posse had gotten started, how he'd come upon the bodies. He changed Thack's ending, making his death swift and heroic.

"He said he was sorry he couldn't make it back."

Sharon's expression—lost in a haze—quickened back to life. "Aces, you said he died fast and before you got there. And now you're giving me his last words? You're lying."

Her face contorted; she twisted her neck. She opened her mouth wide, as though to scream, but instead her words came out as a resigned whisper. "He suffered."

Then she spoke calmly, answering Asa's earlier questions. "The preacher was as tall as me. I think he used raised heels, more than just for a riding boot 'cause he walked all funny, back-to-toe. He had a square jaw and a pale look—the kind you trust. I couldn't but glimpse into his eyes, because they had a preacher's way of seeing straight to sin. Just a pat of hair on his head. No beard, not even grizzle. Aces, do you think he's the devil?"

"Nah. He's just some loser with a sad story. But, you know what? We all got sad stories."

"We sure enough do."

Asa looked out over this desiccated land and concluded that, fundamentally, high and low, all deserts were the same. They could make a man crazy, cutting throats for the sight of blood.

"There's no devil 'cept for us," he said. "I dwelled in an orphan's home 'til I made twelve—long as I could endure the beatings. Then, I hooked up with a wagon rolling off to Texas, when it was Mexican and Indian country. I wound up in a wasteland, mean as any desert, bounding from one ranch to the next, doing chores when they needed a chore boy, which was not often. Some of them owned slaves for their ranch work and not one of them cared a whit for strays.

"So, I took up the way of the gun, running with a band of raiders for a spell. But that didn't set well with me, either. I suppose I'm too full of qualms to go about harming the innocent. Even rustling a cow could drive some of them families beyond hunger.

"By the time I'd fully grown, I ditched the gang, this time off to Laredo, then the Republic of the Rio Grande, where I signed on for the chump job of deputy sheriff. I ended up gunning down punks like me, orphan boys who got banged on the side of the head once too many, hot-blooded and raging to blaze their way to an early damnation. Some gained a name notching their gun belts with the count of their kills. And you know what? They weren't devils, just pitiful cowards. They shot folks in the back, played tricks to outgun one another. Miserable, whimpering creatures—overgrown runts. I sent a great number to Jesus, too many for my own soul's service."

"Asa?" she said, "I don't care." The town and Wynne's Saddlery came into distant view. She looked to her riding companion, suddenly aware of his plan, nodding and grinning. "Kill him."

The town of Safford was a dusty lane hugged by a score of sun-bleached buildings. On the near end, the Skin and Bones Saloon catered to the lucky prospector ladling out bowls of a serviceable chili, enough whiskey to drown in and, on the second floor, handsome and agreeable gals.

Luck ran out at the far end of the road. Capp's Hole, a squat adobe, swapped most any item of passable value for toxic jolts of their homegrown brew. Wretched drunks toppled out of its door while clutching their trousers; their feet were bare, having bartered their boots and belts.

It was late afternoon when Asa and Sharon rode into the saddlery barn. A teenaged boy, his hair a ragged nest of knots, kneeled and dug rocks from a mule's hoof using a hobnail. He glanced at his visitors and nodded, saying, "Aces, Mrs. Cade."

Asa dipped his hat in return. "Chet? Could you see after our horses for a spell?"

Chet pinched up his face. "I'm no livery boy."

"As a favor," Sharon said.

His expression softened when he surveyed Mrs. Cade. Her eyes seemed cried out of tears. She trembled as if a skeletal hand were about to sneak up and snatch her by the shoulder.

Asa said, "Some trouble has been tagging Mrs.

Cade and I need head to find her a safe place for stashing."

Chet frowned. "Don't go sob-storying me. Don't like it. Stealing time is same as stealing."

"I'll pay you a buck," Asa said.

"Now why would you say that? Making out like I don't care. I'll give you an hour."

"An hour until I see the town is clear," Asa said.

Chet gave a jittery nod.

"Bless you," Sharon said.

Chet shook off her attempt to kiss his forehead. He set his face in a scowl and looked away. He took their horses' reins and looped them around the hook of his working post.

Asa asked him, "Chet, did a preacher drop by an hour back?"

"Yes'suh. Sold me a saddle. Dirt cheap, sliced through the belt. I let him know it looked like Tom Jenkins's. He shot me a fiery eye, so I played the mooncalf, saying I wasn't so sure I'd recognize Tom's saddle, not my work. Him thinking I can't spot a stolen saddle. Some preacher. I bought it figgering Tom would pay back the five to get his saddle. Besides, tis my work."

"Where'd he head?" Asa asked.

Chet thumbed at the door. "Out. But it wasn't an hour back. It was more like just now."

Asa gave a grim nod. "Keep the saddle, Chet. Tom's not coming back."

Chet's face became a question mark as he puzzled out the horror.

When riding here, Sharon's horse carried her along. The only choices that needed to be made were done by the creature that dutifully placed one hoof in front of the other. Now, still locked in her prison of pain, she was too dazed to walk a straight line, her shoulder bumping the barn door as she exited. Asa guided her by the elbow. They entered town and he held her close, shielding her from looking down the main road, to where a tall chestnut horse stood hitched in front of Capp's Hole.

A staircase climbed the tall, windowless rear of the Skin and Bones up to a lonely second floor door. Narrow and as rickety as a snake's backbone, it corralled customers and troublemakers into a single file. Asa stood at its base, curled his fingers in his mouth, and issued three sharp whistles. A giant of a man appeared on the upper landing.

"Malc!" Asa waved his arm.

"Aces!" Malc gave a gummy grin. He'd lost his front teeth fighting in the bare-knuckle ring.

Sharon began ascending the stairs with Asa tightly behind her.

"Mrs. Cade? You're with Aces?" Malc said. As a bouncer at a cathouse, human behavior seldom surprised him. It did now, his jaw slack.

"Shut your gawping yapper," Sharon said. "Aces and I didn't come here looking for a romp."

The three stood on the landing. "Malc, Thack is dead. Sharon could be next. I can't think of an abler man to look after a woman."

"Who would want to—?"

"Coffin Jack," she said.

Malc couldn't comprehend fear, even the sensible kind. Asa had heard that once, after being shot, Malc became dangerously annoyed and grabbed the shooter by the gun, squeezing until he crushed every bone in his hand. "Step inside, Mrs. Cade," he said. "Ain't no one coming up these stairs."

–XI–

In its Mexican days, Capp's Hole served as a jail. Hardly more than head high, its small windows were barred. Bullet holes pocked its unpainted mud brick from the stray barrage of firing squads. Hitched in front, a red-brown horse stood eighteen hands tall, a preacher's robe draped over its saddle blanket.

The walls were baked clay. The indoors were an oven, a stifling heat that could sweat away any momentarily sated thirst. Inside, the shadows seemed as heavy as the adobe walls, layered one atop the other, forming thick clots of darkness. Kerosene lanterns—two on the bar counter, two more hanging from the ceiling—provided mere spots of light. Asa scanned the chairs and dark recesses of the booths.

Four nodders sat around a table playing brag for chips of silver ore. A mutt stood atop the bench of a booth slurping up a spilt beer, its head tucked in the shadows, its mangy rear mooning the patrons.

The ancient bartender had more wrinkles than a shrunken head. His skin was translucent, his eyes yellowed. He waved a claw-like hand and clucked his tongue.

"Tut-tut," he said. "House rules. We ask all 'comers to check their firearms behind the bar."

"No," Asa said, patting his holster.

"I said we ask, and I asked."

Asa bent over the bar, grateful for a little more headroom. He set his Stetson to the side. "What you got for a dime?" he asked.

"A pint of our finest gut-kicker."

"Anything worth drinking?"

The bartender uncorked a tall bottle and filled a jigger. He said, "Taos Lightning."

Asa took a taste. It burned his gums. "That's from Taos?"

"The bottle is."

"How many times have you refilled it?"

"Aces!"

Asa whirled. It was Tristan Smith; he'd seen better times. Too many days he'd spent flopped out beneath the desert sun, sleeping off benders. His face had crisped and blistered so often it possessed the leathery look of boiled shoes. He gave a long hacking cough into his hands and clumped up to the bar, one hand gripping his thigh. He braced an elbow against the counter to prop himself up.

"Buy me a corn beer?" he asked.

The bartender held up five fingers. Asa tossed him a nickel.

"And one for my buddy," Tristan said.

The bartender pushed over two mugs of swill.

"You know I could never stomach that corn piss," Asa said.

"That a fact? I can drink both."

Asa slapped a second nickel atop the counter.

Tristan took a greedy gulp. Scum stuck to his upper lip. "How's that dog I sold you?" he asked.

"Still breathing."

"Yup. Smith was good at that. And the horse?"

"Still running."

"Really? He was always so sickly."

"You starved him."

"That a fact? Who could have guessed?"

Asa set his palm flat atop Tristan's mug before he could take another swig. "Amigo, this is important. Have you seen any newcomers drop in here in the last few minutes?"

"Not really," Tristan said, tugging his beer free. "'Cepting for him."

He nodded in the direction of a nook near the door. A stranger sat in the dark, leaning back against the wall, his legs slung up over the bench of a booth. The only things that could clearly be seen were his boots poking out of the stall, and his six-gun on top of the table.

"Tristan?" Asa said. "I need you for an urgent mission."

Tristan screwed up his face with attention.

"Head to the back of Skin and Bones and ask Malc for Mrs. Cade. Tell them to come here. I need her to point out a man before I kill him."

Tristan gazed fearfully at the door, as though sunlight were his enemy.

"I'm counting on you," Asa added.

Tristan gave a firm nod. He clumped along the floor, hand gripping his gimpy leg. He sailed a salute in the direction of the dark booth before opening the door and disappearing into the blinding daylight.

"You see that man in the booth with the gun on the table?" Asa said to the bartender. "Set us up with two drinks that won't give us cause to shoot you." He spun a quarter on the counter.

Asa took out his pistol. He ambled over to the stranger and set his gun on the tabletop alongside the other. Then, he slid into the bench across from him. They spent a long moment in silence, the stranger's hat tipped down, his face a shadow. The bartender set two warm beers on the table.

Asa took a sip. The beer wasn't half-bad. "I see you got your shooting iron ready," Asa said.

"It's a working pistol, my friend," the stranger said. "Can't leave it stuck in a holster. Might grow lazy." His voice was nasal, his words delivered with the fervent pitch of a patent medicine pitchman.

Both Asa and the stranger kept one hand resting on the table, close by their weapons. "What brings you to Capp's?" Asa said.

"The people I hunt come to places like this."

"You hunt people?"

"I suppose I said that."

"You've taken some lives?" Asa asked.

"When the need arises."

"And what brings on this need?"

The stranger chuckled. "Doing them a favor. Life is God's insult."

"Then what's death?"

"The apology."

The stranger leaned forward. He smiled, sucking in his lips as though swallowing a laugh. He had wiry black sideburns that crawled from his temples and swooped to his moustache. His jaw was chisel-sharp, his skin a deep tan, and he had a spark of lunacy in his eyes. He looked nothing like Sharon's description.

Bounty hunter, Asa guessed.

Far off, a shot rang out. Asa bolted to his feet, ran

to and swung open the door. For a moment he stood blinded, then rushed headlong down the town's road toward the Skin and Bones. Outside the saloon, lying on the street, was his carbine. He scooped it up and kept running. By the side of the saloon lay Tristan Smith. A hole in his shoulder gurgled with blood. His mouth gaped open, twisted in an oval of agony, frothing with red foam. Asa knelt beside him, placed a hand on his chest, feeling the wild, rabbity thump of his heart. It stopped.

Malc and Sharon hurried over and, soon, the bounty hunter joined the gathering.

Asa examined a tag of cloth pinned to Tristan's shirt.

I, O, U, ME.

–XII–

Malc saw the note and tucked Sharon under his arm, shielding her as he looked around for the killer, arms tense, fists poised to strike.

The bounty hunter saw the note, expelled a short whistle, and started backing up. He broke into a sprint, heading for Capp's Hole and his horse.

Asa examined Tristan's wound. The shot had come from above, straight down, between his shoulder blades. Jack had ridden up on his horse, firing as he passed his victim. After scanning the dirt, Asa found one set of tracks that paced slowly up to the site of the shooting and then sped off to the north. Seven nails in the shoe.

Asa said, "Malc, take care of…"

"I will," Malc said, interrupting. He jerked his chin. "Go butcher that bastard."

Asa rushed to the saddlery to retrieve his horse. They bounded out of the barn together, galloping off, racing against the waning sun. Given another hour Jack might disappear into the moonless night, this time gone forever.

The bounty hunter rode up alongside the dead body, gun drawn. He jerked his head about, studying the ground, trying to read the tracks. Looking in the direction of Asa, he raced off to chase him down.

Asa followed Jack by the dust his horse kicked up. It lingered over his trail long after he disappeared over the ridges and out of sight, a spectral fingerpost pointing the way forward.

The sinking sun painted the soil a watery red. The shadows of saguaro stretched out, clawing at the dirt, not wanting to be pulled into the night. Stars began winking in the sky. As the ghostly dust of Jack's path faded, something better appeared. Over the ridge was a halo of campfire. Asa pulled on his reins. Hoofbeats sounded from behind.

Asa twisted in his saddle, but before he had his pistol out, he saw the bounty hunter trotting up, rifle at ready.

"'Less'n you draw—my friend—I've no right cause to kill you," he told Asa. "Training my weapon your way is purely a practice of prudence. Don't know you and don't care for you getting skittery on me and welcoming me with an unkind bullet. We need to jaw."

Asa kept his hands spread out wide, fingers tickling the air. "Under the circumstances, talking sounds good."

"Use two of those dancing fingers to draw your pistol and then let it fall."

Asa pinched his pistol, drew it out, and dropped it.

The bounty hunter said, " Seems we both got eyes on the same prize and it's a mighty trophy, indeed. I say it's tough for one man to bring Jack down, so let's the two of us share the perils and divvy the reward. Two grand in bounty—one for you and one for me."

"It's gone up."

"Indeed?"

Asa slowly lowered his arms. "I'm climbing down from my horse," he said. "Dirt's the proper place for sketching out plans."

The bounty hunter nodded an okay. Asa dismounted and took a moment to stretch his legs. The rifle barrel's aim never wavered.

"Asa Powell. Folks call me Aces."

The bounty hunter clucked his tongue. "Heard of ya'. Name's Moreno. I go by Kit."

"Howdy."

Kit swung a leg over his horse and made a smooth drop down, handcuffs jangling on his belt.

Asa supposed the only reason Kit had yet to shoot him came from the needing of help to kill Coffin Jack. With the reward in place, he'd terminate the partnership.

"You can keep the bounty," Asa said. "I'm in it for revenge."

"That no-luck rummy was your friend?" Kit spit air. "And here I figgered you for a huntsman like me. Can't rely on a man out for vengeance, too much boil in the blood. Mammon's a cool passion, the only motive you can trust."

"Not interested. I tried my hand at prospecting. Twenty years looking for that lucky strike that said God smiled my way. Squeezed the gold-lust out of me."

"Then you're alone. Greed's a righteous cause, my

friend, stretching coast to coast. It plucked this territory and me out of the pocket of Mexico. Drew up some boxes to stuff its treasure in, making a *New* Mexico and an Arizona. Christened us Americans. Now we're all greed's children."

"You like your little speeches."

"Indeed I do."

Asa knelt down, waving Kit to come near. He scribbled in the sand, saying, "I'll keep this simple. First, I'll give you time to circle round the far side— find a good spot for sniping. Then, I'll sneak directly up to the camp. I expect to find a trap, a decoy. Maybe a stuffed bedroll. When he makes his appearance, you and me fire."

Kit squinted at the map, deciphering it, nodding.

"Then, there's this," Asa said, making a small *X* in the dirt. When Kit crooked his neck to see, Asa launched a handful of sand into his eyes. He grabbed the rifle barrel and cracked Kit's fingers open to free them from the trigger guard. Kit stood up, slapping the dirt from his face. He felt for his revolver. It wasn't there. A click announced the hammer on his pistol pulling back.

Kit laughed out loud. "Well played, my friend. Now what? Gut-shoot me and leave me to die? A crack of a gun will spook your Mr. Jack."

"The key to your handcuffs," Asa said.

Kit frowned and dug into his pocket, then chucked the key at Asa's feet. Without taking his eyes off of his adversary, Asa knelt and felt for the key. He dropped it down his boot.

"Now take out your handcuffs ," Asa said.

Kit tugged the manacles free from his belt. He

swirled one end as though it were a flail, ready to strike.

"Lock one cuff to the back leg of your horse, then fix the other to your ankle."

Kit did this and then stood up, leaning against his skittish horse, who was trying to yank his leg every which way.

"Stay still," Asa ordered. He pressed the barrel of the revolver at the small of Kit's back, kneeled, and tightened the shackles. Satisfied, he stood up.

Asa said, "Come dawn, keep the sun at your back. About six miles west of here you'll find the Gila River. Where there's water, there's settlers."

"I'm not one to forget, *friend*." Kit gritted a smile. He made a gun out of his fingers and fired.

-XIII-

The darkness was deep, but this stretch of land did not possess the dangers of the Gila Mountains, the sudden drops and poor footholds. Asa walked Tristan, leading him by the reins and weaving between brush.

When Asa crested the ridge to scout Jack's camp, he received a surprise. In the distance, sitting before a fire, was a man wearing black raiments and a flat-brimmed hat. Across from him sat a second preacher dressed in similar robes. One faced Asa, the other presented his back. Both wore holsters with six-guns.

There are two Jacks, Asa thought, but then immediately dismissed this notion. Coffin Jack had simply happened upon a traveling circuit rider.

Asa changed his strategy. He was not going to undertake a surprise assault. Instead—rifle at ready—he mounted Tristan and rode directly to the camp, hoping his appearance would provoke Jack into revealing himself by attacking or running. He was disappointed.

The preacher facing him waved his hand, his sleeve slipping down a tattooed arm. He called out, "Brother, lower your weapon. No enemies here. Come join us and we'll break bread."

The one with his back turned kept silent. He had a tin plate of beans in one hand. The fingers on his other hand danced as though strumming an invisible harp.

Asa halted just outside the rim of the campfire light. The preacher who faced him was clean-shaven. His eyes were intense, stabbing. His nose was crooked, broken. Surely, that would have been something Sharon mentioned.

"Did you not hear me, brother...?" he said, "turn your arm aside, and let us share the Lord's word and bounty." This preacher's hand rested over his gun.

"I'm hunting a man," Asa said.

"Surely not a man of cloth," the second one said—his words matter-of-fact, icy as though his partner had not announced there was a rifle aimed at them. Why hadn't he turned to look at Asa?

Asa said, "I'll ask just once—the both of you—take out your firearms, two fingers on the grips, and toss them aside."

The preacher facing away stopped strumming his harp. He pinched his revolver and hurled it into the dark.

The flat-nosed preacher's hands trembled. He clawed open the strap that held down the cover of his holster. His hand stilled. "You would shoot a child of God if he doesn't give up his weapon? Then how much easier will your crime be if I'm defenseless?"

The preacher whipped his gun out, quickly and professionally, swinging it into perfect aim. Before his enemy's finger could flick the trigger Asa fired, landing a clean blow against his shoulder. The preacher's arm lurched back and his shot went wild, gun flying into the fire.

The other preacher jumped to his feet and bashed

against Tristan, seizing hold of Asa by his free arm. Asa took aim at his attacker with the rifle, but with remarkable strength the preacher grabbed it and yanked him down off of Tristan. Asa landed on top of the preacher and they rolled in the dirt to the brink of the camp flames.

The wounded preacher scrambled backwards into the night.

Asa wrestled, rolling on top of his quarry. He wrapped his hands around the man's throat, squeezing. The man's parsons hat fell off. In the orange flames, Asa could see this preacher clearly: clean-shaven, firm jaw, a pat of hair on the crown of his head—eyes that saw straight through to sin.

Coffin Jack smiled up at Asa, choking out the words with glee, "You shot the wrong one."
Then, Jack's arms relaxed, not fighting back as Asa continued to strangle him. Jack smiled and shut his eyes, taking in a long drink of darkness. When they reopened his pupils veered to one corner, looking over Asa's shoulder.

Asa turned in time to see the other preacher swinging a shovel.

-XIV-

It was an immense, dim abyss. Winter's winds could not measure its depth. Asa dug this hole while looking for gold. Having labored as a bandit, a sheriff's deputy, and an army scout, he'd grown sick of the violent world. Both law and outlaw seemed equally capricious and cruel. His soul felt unraveled; he craved redemption. He searched for it far from humankind, seeking riches, gambling his health and sanity in the desperate life of prospecting.

There he could be alone, hopeless and hoping, waiting for the lucky strike, the deliverance that would prove a merciful God had kept watch over his wretched life, and was now set to bless him with a great bounty. He undertook a futile strategy, certain that gold would be where no one else was looking, as though fortune were a creature, timid and hiding. He dug a single cave deeper and deeper into the dark, until daylight was a tiny distant eye.

So far from the real world, his mine had a climate of its own—temperate. Here his ceiling dripped with the freshest and most refreshing water. Deer and mountain lions came to explore the cave, keeping Asa fed.

One winter's evening, when the high desert was covered with snow and the wind fluted down the throat of his home, a Chiricahua woman stumbled in carrying a newborn child, seeking shelter.

Over the years, Asa had learned the Apache language. Her name was Spring Blossom. The baby she'd been carrying was her half-breed child. The tribe elders had banished her not because they considered the child a sin (The People raised many a white-eye), but rather because Spring Blossom was betrothed to a chief's advisor, so they treated her as a woman of indiscriminate passions.

She was exhausted and feverish. Asa nursed her back to health, spooning her stew made of boiled strips of deer jerky and cactus hearts. The child nursed to plump contentment.

"What do you call your son?" Asa asked.

"He is too young." The People waited for an aspect of personality or distinction to appear before granting a name.

"Let's call him Clement."

"What does that name mean?" she asked.

"It's a name. It has no meaning," Asa said. Her face responded with puzzlement.

One night as Spring Blossom nursed, she offered a breast to Asa. In the shadows she couldn't see him crying as he drank.

They wrapped Clement in a blanket and set him aside.

She pressed her body against his, directing his hand over her pubis. Asa studied it with his fingers. He had never lingered in this place; his only experience had been with prostitutes and he didn't enjoy their services much: their phony moans, their nose-curdling perfumes. On those occasions, the coupling was brusque. He instructed them to "keep quiet and let me do my business".

Now the fur, the mounds, the wetness felt like home. Spring Blossom made soft, guttural noises. He maneuvered his fingers to draw out her sighs, lengthening them, quickening them. She ground against his hand, her excitement increasing. Reaching the brink, she seized hold of his penis and guided it inside of her.

In this darkness they had no boundaries. The fusion of their bodies ignited waves of pleasure, their ecstatic minds flooding with illusory colors. In a world too dark for edges, their hungry spirits became one. She melted with shudders, her muscles clenching in climax. Then, she began to heave her hips against his phallus, moving rapidly, her pleasure again rising and breaking over the top as Asa convulsed, releasing years of dammed-up solitude.

For a winter's month, they had no identities. They were neither Indian nor American. They had no peoples or homeland. They were passion.

A child that's an ephemeral refuge cannot be raised at the borderlands of light and dark. So at winter's end, Asa and Spring Blossom rose out of the cave. Asa packed the scraps of ore he had accumulated over the years and headed to town, where he deposited them in the bank.

At the tribe of the Chiricahuans they received an icy welcome. Even though they married according to tribal ceremonies, Asa represented the white eyes and the cavalry who had penned in their tribe. Since Asa spoke both languages, he took the role of defender for The People, arguing with the army, accusing the Indian agents of graft and the soldiers of brutality.

The army captain refused to recognize Asa's right to voice grievances, stating he was neither Indian nor had an office recognized by the military.

Asa countered with a rambling dogma about the world's peoples. "Being European, you only understand farms and kingdoms. You divide up the land with straight lines. You've taken a nation of hunters and drawn borders around them, sealing them in a box as though the antelope they pursue could be restrained by your invisible boundaries."

The captain half-listened, staring at the back of his hands. "I'm not European," he said. "I'm American."

"There's only Europeans and Indians."

"Then which are you?" The captain let this question linger, certain that with it he had triumphed in their debate. He pinched on a knuckle wart. "They tell me you were once a fine army scout. Too many years in the mines and a man forgets night from day. Nevertheless, in respect for your prior service to our country, I will give you this news in advance. We are about to resettle Spring Blossom's people. You cannot go with her. If you will Christianize your marriage to the satisfaction of the territory of Arizona, she can go with you wherever you choose to settle—that is, excepting the reservation."

When Asa begged Spring Blossom to flee with him, she responded. "Where do we go...back to the cave? That was a moment and it has past. These are forever my people."

Asa promised he would use the meager money he had in the bank to buy a strip of land and build a home. In a year's time, he'd come for her and Clement.

Cheap land was easy to find. He built a one room hut and purchased a dozen sheep, herding them for grazing in the unclaimed pastures left behind by the relocating Chiricahua.

At last, in April of the following year, he rode with a high heart to the San Carlos Reservation to retrieve his family. Once there, Lozen led him to Spring Blossom's grave, dead from cholera.

A pain seared the side of his head, a soreness bucked against his belly. Asa awoke to an upside-down world, staring at horsehide. He was draped over Tristan like a skinned deer. His wrists were bound together, the rope looped under his horse's chest and linked to the knots that secured his ankles. His mouth was stuffed with a rag, which was held in place by a leather lace. He snorted as he breathed.

Jack rode atop a mule, guiding Tristan along. A lantern pole stuck out in front of the beast like a jouster's lance, suspending a kerosene lamp three feet before him.

"I see you've pepped up," Jack said. "Had yourself a mighty clobber."
Jack lacked the harsh drawl of most westerners. He spoke matter-of-factly, as though his mind were elsewhere. "I've been journeying the dead hours to hunt down a village less than acquainted with the famous Aces."

Asa murmured unintelligibly, the wad of cloth muzzling his speech.

"I borrowed this mule from the man you shot," Jack said. "Come the pitch of night, a horse runs too skittish for proper leading, but a good mule will obey orders, follow a lantern or fly you straight over a cliff if you say so with a decent kick."

The fringe of dawn crowned the eastern hills. At this hour the desert winds blew cold, a cruel contrast to the coming inferno.

"You know, I named myself," he said. "In Tucson, after my first kill, I was one of the crowd marveling at the horror of the coffin builder who got buried alive. Someone said, 'this killer is a bloody Jack,' and that insult stung. My work showed a snap of wit and, surely, no blood. I offered up Coffin Jack and it stuck."

The mule joined a rutted wagon trail. "We're riding up on Donalbain," Jack said, "a miner's town. They enforce a brand of justice that runs swifter than the law."

In the meager light of daybreak, the buildings of Donalbain appeared as though they were constructed with playing cards, slanted rectangles that slumped against each other to avoid collapse. Their porches had buckled and their roofs were patchwork of shingles and holes.

With more light the town was even less impressive. Warped boards appeared ready to spring from the buildings. The windows were shuttered or criss-crossed with rough-hewn planks. Faded signs swayed on their hinges. The only sturdy-looking structure was a two-story tall hangman's gibbet. Beneath it a sign warned:

Woe Unto Thee, Malfeezants!

Mongrels trotted in back of Jack and Asa as they passed down Main Street. The wind curled coils of dust behind their motley parade. The only villager up and about was an old woman grinding jeans against a washboard. She halted her work to glare at the passersby.

One ramshackle house was marked with slashing strokes of paint:

Constabulary. Knock Before Shooting.

Jack dismounted, sauntered up to the door and delivered a few solid raps.

"Criminey!" someone said from within. "At this hour, you'd better make this worth the botherment."

The door creaked open. An old man stood in frizzled long johns, one hand buttoning his crotch flap, one hand pointing a revolver. He was scrawny; the kickback on his gun could launch him back into another room. His head was a ball of grey fluff—a tall mop of hair, great bushy eyebrows and an untamed curly beard. His eyes were blotted out by the reflection of the sunrise off of his dust-speckled glasses. He wagged his gun at the man draped over the horse.

"What the fuss?" he said. "Gabs, come see this."

Gabs appeared, also in long johns. He was young and stocky, sported a black horseshoe moustache that arced down below his chin and was waxed at its points. He rested a revolver atop the old man's shoulder, his pop eye set behind the hammer. If he was to fire he'd blind himself and deafen his partner.

"Well, lookie here, Tobin," Gabs said. "We got a man-hunter and his trophy. Come to rent our jail while waiting on the bounty? The cost is five bucks a day up front, and one-ten part of the prize."

Coffin Jack said, "My prisoner shot a fellow preacher, one Reverend Ferris. He was holding this."

Jack held up a hatchet, its blade caked with dried blood and human hairs. "And I found this in his pocket." Jack held out a strip of cloth with letters written in blood.

Gabs gave it a glance. "What do it say, Tobin?"

"I owe you, one preacher," Tobin read.

Gabs nearly leapt out of his skin. "Holy-holy!" he said. "You done snagged yourself Coffin Jack."

Jack whistled and shot up his eyebrows. "You don't say? Well then, the bounty's just as full dead as living. I can save five bucks if you'll treat him to a noontime hanging."

"Hold it there," Tobin said. "You don't get out of paying rent that easy."

Gabs and Tobin cautiously approached Asa, guns aimed and shaking. Gabs drew a knife from his belt. He severed the rope that secured Asa's hands to his feet and heaved him over the horse in a headfirst tumble.

Asa thudded on his back. With bound hands, he clawed the gag from his mouth. He sputtered out grit, gargled some air, and said, "I didn't shoot the reverend. And that man is Coffin Jack."

Jack presented a shocked, wounded look.

"Seems we got a conflict of imputations," Tobin said. "An honest-to-goodness puzzler."

"Tobin was a Pinkerton," his partner said.

"And Gabs was army regular."

"We'll let the Reverend Ferris point out who shot him," Jack said. "He's riding up on my horse. He lagged behind on account of the bullet in his shoulder."

Asa squirmed against his bindings. "No! All right.

Yes, I shot him. Only because he drew on me."

"How about that?" Tobin said. "Stumbled over a fib."

"Sounds like a confession," Gabs said.

"To a shooting that is, not a killing," Tobin pointed out.

"The reverend will tell you who drew first," Asa said.

"Not in this life," Jack said. "I was bluffing. The reverend's not coming. He took a second slug sunk in his forehead."

"Murder it is!" Gabs said.

"All for a better payday," his partner added with glee.

Gabs gave Asa a swift kick in the side. Asa jerked against his bindings, flopping like a beached fish. His sudden stirring startled the lawmen, who shook their pistols at the captive, set to fire.

"Wait!" Asa cried. "Consider this...if I had shot the reverend in the head, then how could I have fallen for that man's bluff?"

The lawmen crossed their weapons, one aimed at Asa, one on Jack.

"I'm Asa Powell," Aces said. "Send word to Safford and you'll find many there who'll vouch for me and one lady—Sharon Cade—who can finger that man as Coffin Jack. You'll have to act quick—she's setting out for Maley to catch the train east."

As Jack's hand crept toward his holster, Gabs and Tobin directed their guns on him.

"Go ahead, draw that gun," Gabs demanded. "Only I want to see it, slow and friendly, like a dove in your hands, no sneaking no finger near the trigger."

"Gabs is a sureshot when provoked," his partner said. "Don't supply him an excuse."

Jack cupped his six-gun in his hands.

"Now, let the dove go," Gabs said.

The six-gun clattered on the porch.

"Gabs, we got ourselves a genuine head-scratcher, here," the old man said. "I say we lock both away while we tally up the evidence."

"I can shoot over to San Simon where they got a Morse telly," Gabs said. "I'll wire Safford, asking that Cade-lady to hurry on by. With a bit of luck we'll crack this nut in time for a six o'clock hanging."

-XVI-

A snug office made up the front room of the town's jail. Sheriff Tobin sat at his desk composing a report. His hand too heavy for the quill, his block letters came out blotched and bleeding. Heaped on the floor beside him was a stack of gun belts confiscated from prior residents whose sojourns were brief and terminal.

In the back, two cells faced one another with the prisoners secured behind bars that ran floor to ceiling. A small slot by the floor allowed in meals. The walls were crusty mortar and jagged stone, hot to the touch and conveying the heat of the sun to create furnace-like chambers.

Tobin filled a tall glass with water.

Asa's throat was parched, his voice hoarse. "Can I have something to drink?"

Tobin said, "You got to earn it."

"How's that?"

"A confession for starts."

Asa spit dust.

The old man's face was mostly lost behind the shaggy growth of his whiskers and the clotted hair dangling from his crown. What remained visible puckered in a frown. He took off his dusty glasses. One eye remained cocked to the side. He plucked it out and plunked it in the water glass.

"How I see it," he said, "it don't matter you getting this Cade-lady fingerpointing Coffin Jack or saying you are Asa Jones or whoever you claim you are. Maybe you and the gal operate in cahoots. Maybe she's a witness of easy virtue. Simplemost choice is to hang the pair of you and let the good Lord thrash the wheat from the chafe."

The sheriff rested the butt of his pistol on his desktop and turned its barrel in the direction of the cells. He said, "Before Gabs and me came to set matters proper, this town was the worst hellhole since Sodom met Gomorrah. Streets packed with blasphemers spewing cusswords like they were popping out tobacco spit. Luscious ladies strumpeting their harlot-y goods beneath the unblushing sun.

"We drove them out, all of them, along with the citizenry who pandered to them. Now all that's left is Gabs, me and four upright folks to preside over our pure and cleansed municipality. Yes, we made a ghost town, and I'm proud of it. The first ever Holy Ghost town. These days them sinners abide in hovels off near the mine and only drop by when we convene a hanging party."

"You got a thunder mug?" Jack asked. He was clenching his pants as though he was a three year old. "I got a powerful need to crap."

"You can relieve yourself in the corner," the sheriff answered.

"Just trying to make your clean-up a bit easier."

The sheriff rose from his seat and grabbed a pie pan. "I tolerate swearing that invokes the excrements. Them is filthy. But do not burn my ears by defaming the good name of the Lord."

At the last moment, Asa realized that Jack wasn't grabbing his pants because he needed to urinate. He had taken off his pants belt.

"Tobin!" Asa shouted.

As the sheriff passed off the plate, Jack looped his belt around the old man's neck, yanking him forward. With the first jerk, the old man's face smashed against the cell's bars, his glasses shattered, shards tinkling on the stone floor. A second crash made him woozy, staggering. Jack grabbed and turned the man, tugging him back up against the bars, the belt crushing his throat. Tobin's arms extended towards Asa.

Asa stretched to reach the sheriff, but was too far away to connect. His desperate effort could only pinch at the tips of his splaying fingers. The sheriff slumped to the ground with Jack twisting the belt ever tighter, finishing the kill. Then, as if nothing had happened, he slid open the loop on his belt, drew it over Tobin's head, and brought it back into his cell. He cinched it around his pants. He folded his hands, weaving his fingers, and sat silently on the cell's bench.

-XVII-

"Not much of a plan," Asa said. "You murdered the sheriff but you're still stuck in his jail."

"Plan?"

Jack seemed offended by the word. "Just had an impulse. I had to end his sermonizing. I saw my belt around his throat and didn't have a choice."

"When his partner returns, he'll hang you."

"Hmm? I hope he doesn't preach at me before the lynching. I couldn't tolerate that." Jack placed the heels of his hands against the bars, pressing them as though puzzled by why they simply didn't fall over.

"Why didn't you kill Sharon Cade?" Asa asked. "She saw you, she could identify you."

"A moment of weakness, I guess. I wanted to, but then she gave me a glass of water. I let her be, a mistake I'll rectify—when I escape."

"Escape? And how do you plan to do that?"

"Plan?"

Jack closed his eyes, tilted his head. Then he got up and pressed his cheek against the warm stone wall.

"I like the heat. I lived through the Cariboo Rush of '62 up in the Northern Rockies. It got so cold, that I once had to shave the socks from my feet. I lost my toes to frost. In those ravenous winters, many a fellow prospector trained a hungry eye on their partners. But not all of us got eaten."

He pushed back from the wall. His head cocked to the side. He whispered, "Someone's coming."

Asa listened. The tramping of horse feet stopped at the side of the jailhouse, followed by soft, padding footfalls, no jingle of spurs.

The front door opened—Lozen.

She clutched a bone-handled knife to her side, her arm tense and ready. She surveyed the cells, the dead sheriff.

She walked over to Jack, firing off a fierce stare. Jack pressed his face against the bars, returning her stare and adding a brazen smile. She spoke in Apache, saying, "I've come to tell you...you will take no more of the lives of my people."

Asa translated.

She told Asa, "I followed Tristan's trail to this door. I could see he was being led by a mule. I suspected Jack. The council of The People have ruled on his fate."

"The Chiricahuans have passed judgment," Asa told Jack.

"Coffin Jack has inspired a sweeping fear among the white eyes," Lozen continued. "Great posses and bands of army scouts have hunted him. In their terror, the white eyes have often left my tribe alone. When tragedy strikes, they don't look to us for accusations. This season of peace has been brief, but profound. He is your evil. As long as he does not again take the life from one of The People, the council will allow Coffin Jack to live. I will set him free."

"Lozen, you can't," Asa said.

"This is what the elders have decided. I cannot

help you to escape, Asa. Unless Jack has passed far away, you will kill him."

Although Asa had stopped translating the message, Jack drank with glee the agony in Asa's expression.

"Did you deliver my message to Clement?" Asa asked.

"He doesn't know you," she said.

Lozen took the key from a peg on the wall. She placed it in the lock of Jack's cell. "You must no more take the lives of our tribe. You may go."

Lozen hurried to the door, where she paused to give Asa a parting glance. The fury she maintained in her every expression—for a moment—softened. She swung the door open, hid from the sun while carefully listening for the sound of townsfolk, anyone who might question the presence of an Indian at the jailhouse. After hearing nothing, she peeked out and then slipped along the wall, ducking into the alley. She leaped atop her horse.

"She said the condition for your release is that you don't kill another Indian," Asa said, "and you will leave here—not killing me."

Jack leaned back on his bench in no seeming hurry. "I promise I won't kill no more reds," he said. "That sport never sat right with me."

Jack turned the key and swung his cell open. Stepping over Tobin's corpse, he proceeded to the jailhouse door, opened it, and stared out at the blinding day and near-empty town. He took the water glass containing the false eye and downed its contents. The eyeball reappeared, cupped between his lips. With a puff it clattered onto the floor, covered in his spit.

After collecting his gun belt and hatchet, he returned to Tobin, confiscating the handcuffs from the sheriff's belt.

He said, "When I was a child, my parents died while traveling between watering holes. I got rescued, just a tiny papoose, and was raised by the Yavapai. Before long my new family got butchered by Indian-hating vigilantes, who then took me to their care. I've seen the cruelty of Indians, soldiers, outlaws, and cannibals. But the righteous zealots, them are the genuine savages."

Then, he used his hatchet to carve a line along the old man's forehead, down his temples, continuing back around the skullcap. Little by little, he pried free the scalp.

Lifting the trophy over his head, Jack rose to his feet, droplets of blood raining down his face. He turned his pistol on Asa, saying, "I've never favored the gun, takes too long to teach it who to shoot. The hatchet knows where to settle my rage, sure as a blow from my hand. With a hefty swing, me and the blade are one with the blood. A proper killing ought to be personal. But in a pinch," he pulled back the hammer, "I'll make an exception and blast away. Stand back."

He nodded with the gun's barrel to underscore his demand.

Asa backed against the wall.

Coffin Jack tossed him the sheriff's handcuffs.

"Now add one end to your wrist," Jack ordered.

Asa snapped the bracelet around his wrist, squeezing it tight before being asked.

"Slide the chain between the bars and cuff the other end to the sheriff."

Asa hesitated, so Jack drew back the hammer. Asa nodded in surrender, crouched next to the bars, seized Tobin by the hand, and cuffed himself to the corpse.

Jack tossed the sheriff's scalp to the back of the cell. "Revenge bait," he said, "for your lynching party. When the deputy returns, this hank of skin and hair will boil up some extra fury for your hanging."

Jack set the key in Asa's cell door. "However, you do got one chance. If you can separate the sheriff's hand from his wrist in time, you can jingle free your cuffs and run. I recommend using your teeth. Whatever you do, when you finish, I'll be far gone."

Jack holstered his gun and gave a toothy farewell smile. He backed away, pausing at the door.

"If you do get away, I'll be killing you soon enough." He nodded, adding, "I owe you."

-XVIII-

Asa waited for the sounds of Jack mounting a horse and taking off, then skid his boot up the wall and shook his foot. The handcuff key he'd pinched from Kit Moreno tumbled out. It was gnawing at his foot. He used it to pop open the manacles.

From the office he gathered his belt and six-shooter. Cracking open the barrel, he found it had been emptied. Rather than scrounging drawers for the right caliber, he filled it with the ammo from his bullet loops. He slapped the barrel closed, gave it a spin, and slid the gun into his holster.

Tristan stood tied to a watering trough. He'd been better treated than Asa, but then Tobin and Gabs expected the horse to survive the day. Asa sailed a blanket over his horse's back, smoothed it, and then heaved a saddle on top. He tugged the buckle tight. Tristan looked pained; Asa's obsession was taking its toll. He cupped Tristan's snout in his hands and leaned head to head. When he thought they had reached an understanding, he gave Tristan's forelock a ruffle.

Asa slopped some trough water over his face, then sunk his boot into the stirrup and swung up his leg up and over his horse. He tugged on the reins and Tristan stuttered backwards. It was only then that he heard someone riding up behind him, a horse kicking dirt.

Asa spun his horse and drew his gun in one motion. In doing this he caught Gabs with his revolver still in its holster. Back from a hard ride, the deputy was powdered with dust, his drooping moustache appeared gray. His fingers tickled the air, uncertain what to do.

"I urge you to stay that hand," Asa said.

Then, to his side, he heard the boxlock action of a shotgun being cracked and cocked. Asa slipped his gun into its leather sheath, patted Tristan's shoulder and dismounted.

He turned to greet Kit Moreno.

"Hello, friend," Kit said. "I told you I don't forget."

Asa unbuckled his gunbelt. It dropped to the dirt.

"Why are you out here?" Gabs demanded. "Where's Tobin?"

Asa tilted his head in the direction of the jailhouse door. Gabs rushed off.

Kit bobbed his aim between head and belly, undecided where to shoot. "Your chica, Mrs. Cade, had run off to catch the train," he said.

"Fortunate I was on hand to come vouch for you. Wait until morning for the sunlight to point the way? Don't you think I can suss out west from the North Star?"

Gabs returned with his face flushed red. His gun was out and ready to fire. "He killed Tobin, slaughtered and scalped him in his own jail."

"That was Coffin Jack," Asa said. "Don't you think it's suspicious your other prisoner is long gone?"

"Oh, it was Jack, all right," Kit said. "Sheriff, I came here to make an identification. This man before you is Coffin Jack."

"If it was me, how'd I get loose? Where's your other prisoner? Where's the hatchet?"

Gabs smacked the butt of his gun against Asa's temple, silencing him.

Six PM: the perfect hour for a lynching.

The heat of day had broken. With the miners' five-to-five shift over, they had gotten the word and hustled over to Donalbain, desperate for some spirited entertainment. This hanging promised to be a memorable one—Coffin Jack, Sheriff Tobin's killer. Gabs charged a full ten cents for a spot in the front of the crowd. As proof of payment, the patrons wore white ribbons pinned to their vests. Kit Moreno lurked at the back fringe of the crowd, his face stone stiff.

They'd constructed the gallows as a bona fide stage, two stories tall, its hanging frame a horizontal beam suspended between towering pillars of ponderosa timber. The platform rested eight feet above the street, the space beneath a puppet theater where dangling men danced their farewell performance.

A ladder poked up through the trap in its deck. Asa's leg irons were removed so that he could climb. He clambered up the ladder with a rickety gait, his hands unable to aid in his ascent. His wrists were knotted in front of him, his hands wrapped in cloth, sealed together in a forced prayer. His mouth was gagged to ensure his final words were his only words. He kneeled against the top rung, most of his body above the platform, and his feet were positioned two rungs below. Gabs fixed the noose around his neck, tightening the loop, leaving just enough slack for breathing.

For the price of a dollar, a spectator gained the right to kick out the ladder. The rope's slack was enough for a four foot drop. With a proper jerk, Asa's neck would snap and there would be only a little squirming. Otherwise, the audience thrilled to a slow strangulation with a lengthy, lively jig.

With his prisoner secured, Gabs waved his gun around, advising Asa, "It's time to suck up your courage and die with proper manners like a good sport. If you try something foolhardy, I'll wing you, just enough to wound while keeping certain you'll stay jittering through your sendoff. Can't disappoint the crowd."

The gathering numbered three score, a vast muttering collection of soot-covered miners, ladies of the evening, several petticoats, and a young child in a pudding cap.

In such moments of tension, Gabs sucked on his moustache. He cleared his throat, wiped the moisture from his bristles, and then waved his arm for silence. He switched his ten-gallon hat for a formal derby. It was a prime moment to sermonize.

He called out, "You all know me—Gabriel Ramirez—once deputy, now sheriff. Some call me Gabs. I've always promised you folks high quality mob justice, a vow I take honor in upholding."

In the desert beyond the crowd, Asa could see a rider approaching, his horse kicking up thunderheads of dust.

"Some of you sinners criticized me and Tobin when, in a frenzy of moral fitness, we booted you far from your homes. Now you slink back here to celebrate the virtues of retribution, the godly spectacle that is the fruit of righteous wrath. This man has killed my partner, my friend, my guiding spirit."

All eyes rested on Gabs and Asa. They didn't notice the man dismounting from Sheriff Tobin's horse. He drew a hatchet from its sheath.

Asa grunted into his gag. He pinched and twitched at the ribbon of rag that bound his hands together, slowly unraveling it.

"This pitiless monster that kneels at the altar of his destruction has shortened the days of all too many a child of God. One virtuous citizen, Kit Moreno, undertook a furious charge to be here and deliver him to the judgment he has so well earned."

Moreno tipped his hat. Jack raised his hatchet.

Gabs continued. "Some say that the Lord waits ready with forgiveness. They think God is weak, can't hold a grudge. I say the Almighty's fist can squeeze out of any grudge the fullness of its fury. This man before you shows what comes of them who transgress divine law. Alas and alack! They wind up jerked to judgment, fluttering at a rope's end, gasping for one more breath before they begin their eternal stay in a pit of unquenchable fire."

Asa freed his fingers, snatched at his gag. Gabs saw what he was doing and unbound the gag himself.

"Do you have any final words?" Gabs asked.

"Coffin Jack!" Asa said.

Jack slid his hatchet along Kit's throat, unleashing

a wash of blood and spraying those nearby. The crowd erupted in cries and screams, men and women jostling, shoving one another.

Gabs was slow to react. By the time he'd drawn his gun Jack had fired and missed his target. The sheriff dove to the deck of the gallows. One of the scattering mob members bumped against the ladder. Asa's feet tottered, struggling for balance. Gabs popped off shots, not expecting to hit Jack, but trying to keep his opponent from taking aim.

Jack clutched a woman to his chest, using her as a shield, returning fire.

Gabs crawled to the lip of the platform; he was wearing a scabbard. With his wrists still tied, Asa cupped his fingers like tiny flippers to pluck out the knife. He flipped the jagged edge, the handle tucked between his fingers, the blade slipping beneath the cord that bound his wrists. Asa twisted his hands and sawed at the rope.

The lady he held hostage fought to be free and Jack's aim swayed. He shoved her to the ground and shot her, then ducked for cover beneath the gallows, firing up, popping bullets through the planks.

Gabs squatted, returning fire down between his legs and through the platform. One of Jack's bullets found its mark, striking Gabs in the chest; he clutched at the burning wound, his lung gargling a froth of blood. Gabs dropped face-down.

With his hands free, Asa raised the blade over his head and began to carve through the line supporting the noose.

Jack unloaded a chamber, blasting a foot of the ladder off. Asa fought to keep from falling.

After shucking the empty shells from his revolver, Jack thumbed in a fresh batch.

Asa shuffled for balance and support, the noose crushing his windpipe.

Gabs dipped over the edge of the platform, head upside-down, set to fire below. Before he could shoot, Jack pivoted and unloaded a line of bullets through the wood, discharging his last shot point blank into Gabs's face.

Jack swung his hatchet, chopping into the rail of the ladder. Asa's foothold, already tenuous, gave way. The ladder split, tumbling to the dirt. Asa seized the cord above his neck with one hand as he dropped through the trap in the platform. The slack above him gave way, wrenching his arm. With his other hand he continued to hack through the rope as he dangled in front of Jack.

The killer raised his hatchet, but Asa swung and kicked him backwards. With a final few rasping strokes, Asa sliced through the remaining twine that held him in suspension. He dropped to the ground, landing crouched on three points, directing his blade at Jack.

A citizen approached with a rifle barrel raised. Jack blasted him in the chest. Asa took the moment of distraction to seize Gabs's gun from its place in the dirt. Jack wheeled, clicked at Asa with an empty gun. Then, he charged into the crowd, swinging his hatchet to make certain they scattered. He stepped on top of Kit's corpse to mount his horse. Still gasping for breath, Asa fired off several wild shots as Jack sped away.

-XX-

With its lawmen dead and the crowd dispersed, Asa had his run of Donalbain. Those who might consider confronting him steered clear as though the noose still dangling from his neck was the lit fuse on a stick of dynamite.

As darkness descended, Asa gathered together the stray bits of his life: his pistol, his horse and saddle. When he couldn't find the remainder of his possessions, he stole a new Stetson, a clunky but working repeater rifle. He drank water until his stomach ached. He broke a window and swiped a tray of biscuits. When at last he mounted Tristan, he shucked his noose.

"Come on, boy," Asa said. "We've got another hard ride ahead."

Tristan peeled back his upper lip, emitting something between a snort and a hiss.

In the final, vanishing moments of dusk, Asa sped off into the flatlands. He didn't need to track Jack; he knew his quarry's destination.

Jack had regretted not killing Sharon, vowing to rectify the error. She would be boarding the morning train in Maley.

Although unacquainted with this stretch of land, Asa's path was simple: head straight south until he met up with the railroad and the follow the tracks to town. He and Tristan passed beneath a glittering crown of stars. The ground below invisible, the passage became plodding, sage and ocotillo scratched against his loyal horse's legs. The silhouettes of saguaro surrounded them, limbs lifted as though they were a tribe in surrender. A small one seemed like a child reaching out.

"Clement."

At midday this land would be an anvil and Asa a metal shoe, freshly fired in the kiln, set to be beaten by the hammering sun. At night the wind lashed with a mordant chill. Each time Asa shut his eyes, the landscape of his dreams matched the darkness of the terrain and, soon, he became uncertain when he was sleeping. He lashed himself to the saddle to keep from falling off.

He awoke as Tristan shuffled against a rise of chipped slate, the rail line. They turned to the west.

The Southern Pacific line ran from San Diego to El Paso. Dotting the vast, mean wasteland was a series of one-hut watering stations along with several villages that braved the nothingness, including Maley. Here, the train made a full stop with stagecoach service to Solomonville, Fort Bowie, and Tombstone.

With the first winking sliver of the sun as it crested the rocky Dos Cabezas, Asa beheld the long tether of rail heading to the Maley station. The town's streets lay spread out in the form of Tic-Tac-Toe, two avenues crossing two others. At its southeastern edge was the depot. Beyond the borderline of rail was unending desert.

In the distance, a locomotive coughed up sooty smoke. It would arrive in Maley in minutes. Asa thumped Tristan who responded with a trot.

———————————

The white face of the depot's wall clock mirrored the blaze of the sun. Because it ran slow each day, the station master popped open the clock glass and nudged the minute hand to *XI*. He cranked the weighted chain around its drum, and then tipped the pendulum into motion. The teeth of its gear clacked against the catch, ticking off the seconds.

Too large to find comfortable seating, Malc draped himself across the station's wooden bench. A dead cigarette dangled from the corner of is lips. He impatiently ground fist into palm. Sharon Cade stood in a bustled petticoat, her eyes cast in the direction of the approaching train.

The air already had the tingle of the scorching day ahead. Malc cleared his dust-dry throat. Sharon smudged away a crumble of dirt that crusted along the corners of her eyes.

The whistle heralded the train's arrival: a lead engine, a coal car, two cargo flats stacked with tall bundles of rails and ties for the construction beyond El Paso. At the rear were two passenger cars. The brakes spit steam, the metal wheels squealed as the engine skid to a halt.

With her attention fixed on the train, Sharon didn't see Asa arrive. Malc recognized Tristan's snort and cocked an eye his way. The giant clambered to his feet.

"Aces?" he said, as though it couldn't be.

Asa dismounted and gave him a firm handshake.

"Aces!" Sharon greeted him with a kiss.

"Bad news," Asa said. "Coffin Jack, he's coming for you."

Malc balled his sledgehammer fists, looking about for someone to punch.

"Let's hope he's running late," Asa continued. "If not, we'll stop him here. There's no way he could catch the train before Maley. I'll hang outside the rail car with my rifle, making sure Jack doesn't get onboard. Malc, you ride with Sharon, guard her. See her to Teviston and then hop the return train back. Take this."

Asa offered him his revolver.

Malc sneered. "You know I don't...I mean, a gun don't equal a solid punch. Can't even swing it as a proper billy."

"I know how to work one," Sharon said, snatching the pistol.

"How long does the train stop here?" Asa asked the station master.

"Three minutes precise," he said. "We've a schedule to keep. You'd better hop to it."

One couple disembarked. Malc and Sharon stepped on to the tread board, then up on to the vestibule platform of the end car. A porter toted their baggage. Asa took post behind the train, choosing an angle where he could see someone approaching from either side. He tucked his carbine rifle under his arm, the barrel in his hand, relaxed but ready to drop into action.

Malc came out the back door of the cab, stepping onto the viewing deck. He delivered an all-is-well wave. With that done he disappeared inside, and then...nothing. Spits of steam blasted from the sides of the locomotive. The arriving couple spoke with the station master. A boil of hawks spiraled in a giddy updraft. A dray horse hauled a wobbly carriage loaded with scrap down the main avenue.

No one drew near to the train from the desert or town. Asa looked to the distance for a dust trail announcing an approaching horse. The only dust came with the wind that seemed to be exhaled out of the sun.

He began to wonder if he was wrong. Perhaps, Jack's vow to kill Sharon meant nothing. It should mean nothing now that a whole crowd at Donalbain had seen his face.

Asa squinted at the station clock. The station master glared at his pocket watch.

With a jolt Asa realized that more than three minutes had passed. He slung his hand inside his rifle's trigger guard and hurried to the front of the train, seizing its metal ladder and entering the conductor's cab. There he found the engineer and assistant with their throats carved open, lying in a joint pool of their blood.

Some rocks shuffled behind him. He wheeled, ready to shoot. A twelve-year old boy caked head-to-foot in coal dust rose from the fuel bin. He trembled, tears eroding the grit beneath his eyes.

"He killed 'em," the boy said. "Cut their throats."

"Can you run this train?" Asa asked.

"I know how to start and stop. Ain't nothing to steer."

"The killer's headed to the passenger car. I won't hazard a shootout in a packed coach, so I'll be chasing him to the desert, but I'll need you to speed the train far from here. You've got to get this train moving or more will die."

The young boy examined the dials. "The pressure's been bled. It'll take a couple of minutes."

A series of gunshots rang out from the rear of the train.

Asa leaped down from the engine, scrabbled among the gravel, gained his footing, and hurtled headlong past the coal and freight cars.

With a hatchet in one hand, a pistol in his other, Coffin Jack booted open the coach door. The stunned travelers were frozen in their seats as he fired a shot through the ceiling. The passengers bounded into the aisles, one atop of another, with Jack gunning down those closest to the exit.

In the next coach over Malc leaped to his feet, shoved Sharon aside, dipped his head, and tramped toward the source of the shots. Although Malc had picked up money from bare-knuckle boxing, his fighting skills were neither science nor sweet. His fists hung low, his chin a clean target if someone got near. Not many did.

His prey, Coffin Jack, now stood at the far end of an aisle—which was carpeted with writhing humans—brandishing a half-full gun. Malc stomped over the passengers, all of his muscles drawn tight, from his neck that seemed ready to spring out like a Jack-in-the-box, to his fists that churned air.

Jack fired three rapid shots, closely spaced. The first whizzed past Malc's ear; the second grazed his neck; the third caught his throat. Malc gargled and disgorged blood like a dragon spitting flames. He used one hand to cover his gushing wound, while the other bashed Jack hard enough to send him crashing back against the cabin door.

Jack responded by whipping his hatchet. Malc jerked his arm back so that the blade merely cleaved air. Panicking passengers squeezed and crawled around Malc, one between his legs. The giant tottered and grasped the back of a bench. He experienced a sensation he'd never felt before: weakness. A sheet of blood soaked his shirt down to his pants. He swayed woozily. He refocused and drew his fist back, leaning to within striking range.

As Jack raised his hatchet, Asa shoved the door open behind him. Jack had a two part response to those who attacked from behind. He swiped the hatchet down and backwards, hitting Asa in the kneecap with the blunt end, causing him to crumple to his knees. Then, Jack pivoted, swinging the blade to bring it home against Asa's throat. Before he made contact Sharon fired her weapon, once, and well-aimed. The recoil kicked her hands. The slug pierced Jack's side—a ripe, blooming belly wound.

As she aimed a second shot, Jack shoved his way past Asa out the coach door. He leaped off the boarding platform of the train.

With kneecap shattered, Asa hobbled to platform where he saw Jack bleeding, staggering east into the desert. With Tristan as his legs, he'd be able to run Jack down and finish it right there.

Just as the train jerked into motion, he climbed off the platform and stumbled toward the depot, using his rifle as a cane. Before mounting his horse, he looked back. In the flash of space between the engine and coal car, he saw that Jack had reversed direction. He was now heading back toward the train.

The locomotive ambled on, slowly accelerating. Beyond the flickering gap between the coal car and freight, Asa could see Jack's figure. He would climb aboard the train. Asa raised his rifle and wrenched his busted knee into a rigid position. He fired between the two freight cars at the strobing image, and hit metal. He cocked and again fired between the freight and the first passenger car, missing a second time. Jack reached out to seize a handhold of the train.

The first passenger car passed. Asa fired once more. Jack had boarded the platform and fired back. Asa was certain he had failed. Even with Tristan at a gallop, even if they could catch up with the train, with his lame leg he could never leap aboard.

It was only after the final carriage had passed that Asa saw Jack splayed out in the dirt beside the tracks. He had fallen from the train. There was a bullet hole in his forehead.

-XXI-

Exhausted and broken, a feral anger still surged through Asa's veins. The townsfolk—sure of the sound of gunfire, unsure of what had happened—kept their distance. Asa draped Coffin Jack's body over Tristan's back and rode into the desert to begin his journey home. He had never been in this for the reward, but the sizeable bounty could help him repair his life. Would his sheep be alive?

He would hire a ranch hand, at least until his leg recovered, but then...why stop there? He could afford a better ranch with a proper stretch of grazing land; maybe add a room or two to his shack. He could make a home for Clement. No, why would his son want to live with him? Clement was a useless fantasy, someone he barely knew, not even family. Asa had no one. Even if Clement did come to live with him, he'd be treated by the white-eyes as a half-breed. His son's people were the Chiricahua. On the other hand—the San Carlos Reservation made for a horrid existence, being starved to death on a pestilent tract of land unfit for hunting or farming.

Asa had heard of schools for Indians. Perhaps, he could pay to send Clement to one where he could be among his own, but still get a civilized education. Asa snorted at this idea, scolding himself for even using that word. He had heard of the beast called civilization and seen the lie of its existence. Asa had enough of enlightened society during his childhood—the stern and hypocritical judge who managed the orphan asylum, and the good townsfolk who robbed him of his family.

At age ten, when Asa first ran away from the brutality of the St. Louis Home for Boys, he met up with a pair of fugitive slaves on the road. They tried to convince him to join them in the far-off Indian territories, Mexican lands so far from Mexico that everyone could be their own law. If you are your own law, they told him, no one owns you. Asa declined, instead stealing his way to Western Missouri and his hometown.

His brother had grown to six years of age. Dressed in Sunday's best—white shirt, a vest, and a plump white bow—he lingered outside the church after the morning's service, while his guardians stood joking with the pastor. Asa whistled to his brother from his hideout in the nearby bushes. The child, at an age where he heeded the call of whistles, answered the summons.

"I'm your brother," Asa told him. "Those people are not your parents. They killed mom and dad and they sent me away. But we can be together again. We can escape—come with me..."

Clement.

His brother screamed. Asa was dragged away by a church alderman. The town council met and decided to ship him back to the asylum with the warning that if he ever returned, he'd be sent to the state pen being built in Jefferson City.

One year later he ran away again, returning to

discover that his brother and his guardians had moved on. No one would tell him where they'd gone.

With this second homecoming, the townspeople didn't care to punish him or ship him off to prison. They showed no concern as to whether or not he returned to the orphanage. They simply ignored him. Asa headed back to the boy's home, its cruelties were all he had, staying another year until he could take it no more.

The first sign of tragedy was the empty sheep pen. Smith sat in front of its wide-open gate, tall on his haunches. Mouth gaping and grinning, tongue waggling, he radiated an unapologetic bliss.

Asa followed a herd of hoofmarks over the ridge, where he passed by a half-dozen scattered arrows. Thirty yards more and he encountered a dead sheep, a bullet hole in its temple. Who would shoot a sheep?

Asa dismounted and knelt next to its corpse. Although its nose felt cold, maggots had not yet bloomed; it had probably been dead since morning. There, in the sand behind its remains, were hand and moccasin prints. An Apache crouched here for cover from gunfire, launching arrows until his shield took a bullet to the brain, but then why wasn't the Indian shot?

He paced in the direction of the arrows, reasoning that the ones strewn about the ground were the ones that missed (they had flown the furthest). Before reaching them he found the marks of horseshoes, a couple of spent cartridges, and a dribble of blood.

When the gunman was struck by an arrow, he bolted off on his horse. Asa followed the trail down into a ravine to where he encountered a cavalry soldier lying in the dirt, one arrow in his gut, another broken off in his chest. He clutched the shattered shaft in his hand.

He had been face to the sun since daybreak, his skin red and blistered, his eyes puffy slits.

"Aces," he said.

Asa didn't recognize him. He hardly looked human. "I'm here," Asa said.

He fed the soldier some water from his canteen, but even a spit's worth made him cough like he was drowning.

"I'd heard you'd been trailing Coffin Jack," the soldier said. "So I showed up at your place looking for you, to see if you could use an extra gun. I came across the Chiricahua raiding your sheep. I tried..."

He gurgled up something that looked too thick to be blood.

Asa sat next to him and took the man's hand. The soldier cried. They said nothing more. After a time he stopped breathing.

Asa had told Lozen the flock was theirs if he didn't return from chasing down Jack. Maybe that was why she'd left him in the jailhouse. She thought he was dead.

Now the Chiricahuans had killed a soldier. This would ignite another round of revenge and if neither side backed down, an all-out war.

Asa thought, *maybe there's another choice*. He muttered a prayer he hadn't used in fifty years, then hacked into the man's corpse and dug out the arrows. He sliced open the dead man's throat. After tearing out a piece of cloth, he spelled out in blood *I, O, U*, but couldn't conjure up how to finish it, so he wrote: *NOTHING.*

He would haul the body of Coffin Jack off and

dump it where it would never be found: at the bottom of his old mine.

What was it that Lozen had said? As long as Coffin Jack lived, the cavalry left the Indians alone.

By keeping Jack alive, Asa could buy time for The People, a brief respite from hostilities. Maybe a fleeting moment of peace was the most one could hope for from this life.